DISCARD

CULTURAL MOSAIC

The Middle Eastern American Experience

Sandy Donovan

Twenty-First Century Books · Minneapolis

> This book takes a broad look at Middle Eastern Americans. However, like all cultural groups, the Middle Eastern American community is extremely diverse. Each member of this community relates to his or her background and heritage in different ways, and each has had a different experience of what it means to be Middle Eastern American.

USA TODAY®, its logo, and associated graphics are federally registered trademarks. All rights are reserved. All USA TODAY text, graphics, and photographs are used pursuant to a license and may not be reproduced, distributed, or otherwise used without the express written consent of Gannett Co., Inc.

USA TODAY Snapshots®, graphics, and excerpts from USA TODAY articles quoted on back cover and on pages 14–15, 22–23, 34–35, 41, 42–43, 45, 53, 54–55, and 66–67 © copyright 2011 by USA TODAY.

Copyright © 2011 by Lerner Publishing Group, Inc.

All rights reserved. International copyright secured. No part of this book may be reproduced, stored in a retrieval system, or transmitted in any form or by any means— electronic, mechanical, photocopying, recording, or otherwise—without the prior written permission of Lerner Publishing Group, Inc., except for the inclusion of brief quotations in an acknowledged review.

Twenty-First Century Books
A division of Lerner Publishing Group, Inc.
241 First Avenue North
Minneapolis, MN 55401 U.S.A.

Website address: www.lernerbooks.com

Library of Congress Cataloging-in-Publication Data

Donovan, Sandra, 1967–
    The Middle Eastern American experience / by Sandy Donovan.
       p.   cm. — (USA TODAY Cultural mosaic)
    Includes bibliographical references and index.
    ISBN 978-0-7613-4087-4 (lib. bdg. : alk. paper)
    1. Middle Eastern Americans—History—Juvenile literature. 2. Middle Eastern Americans—Social life and customs—Juvenile literature. I. Title.
E184.M52D66 2011
973'.0494—dc22   2009045922

Manufactured in the United States of America
1 – DP – 7/15/10

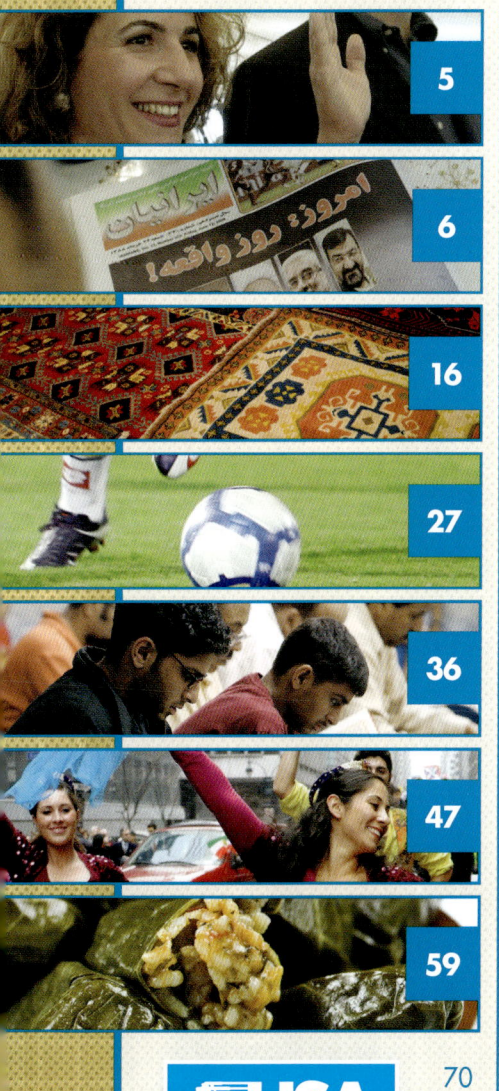

INTRODUCTION:
5 FROM THE MIDDLE EAST TO THE UNITED STATES

CHAPTER 1:
6 CONNECTING THROUGH LANGUAGE AND LITERATURE

CHAPTER 2:
16 MIDDLE EASTERN INFLUENCE ON ART AND MUSIC

CHAPTER 3:
27 EXCELLING IN SPORTS

CHAPTER 4:
36 RELIGIOUS FAITHS

CHAPTER 5:
47 CELEBRATING HOLIDAYS

CHAPTER 6:
59 TASTES OF THE MIDDLE EAST

70	FAMOUS MIDDLE EASTERN AMERICANS
72	EXPLORE YOUR HERITAGE
74	MIDDLE EASTERN AMERICAN SNAPSHOT
75	GLOSSARY
76	SELECTED BIBLIOGRAPHY
77	FURTHER READING AND WEBSITES
78	INDEX

Leila Nessralla, an immigrant from Lebanon, takes the citizenship oath during a ceremony in Massachusetts.

USA TODAY
CULTURAL MOSAIC

INTRODUCTION:
FROM THE MIDDLE EAST TO THE UNITED STATES

Middle Easterners have been coming to the United States in large numbers since the late 1800s. At that time, Christians from Lebanon and Syria began fleeing their homelands to escape poverty and discrimination (unfair treatment) for their religious beliefs. Christians follow the teachings of Jesus Christ. Lebanon and Syria were then part of a Muslim empire. Muslims follow the teachings of Muhammad, who founded the religion of Islam in the A.D. 600s.

Many twentieth-century Middle Eastern immigrants were Muslims or Jews. (Jews follow the religion of Judaism, a system of beliefs and practices set forth in the Hebrew Bible—which Christians call the Old Testament.) Violent conflicts such as the Arab-Israeli War of 1948–1949 and the Iranian Revolution of 1979 prompted more immigration from the Middle East. In the early 2000s, at least one million Middle Eastern Americans live in the United States.

Middle Eastern Americans come from many different backgrounds. They have roots in Turkey, Lebanon, Syria, Jordan, Israel, Palestine, Saudi Arabia, Kuwait, Bahrain, Qatar, the United Arab Emirates, Oman, Yemen, Iran, Iraq, Egypt, or Libya. They may speak Arabic, Persian, Hebrew, or other languages. And they may practice Christianity, Islam, Judaism, or other religions.

What traditions shape the lives of Middle Eastern Americans? And what contributions have they made to U.S. society? Let's explore Middle Eastern American culture and find out!

CHAPTER 1:
CONNECTING THROUGH LANGUAGE AND LITERATURE

Middle Eastern Americans speak many languages. Many people who come from the Middle East speak Arabic. People from Iran speak Persian, and people from Turkey speak Turkish. In Israel, Hebrew is the most common language. Each of these languages has its own alphabet. So immigrants to the United States who don't already know English learn a new language and a new alphabet.

Many Middle Eastern immigrants learn some English before moving to the United States. In some Middle Eastern countries, such as Jordan and Lebanon, English is widely spoken. And in others, such as Iran and Saudi Arabia,

Adult students learn English as a second language at a community college in Maine. Some Middle Eastern immigrants learn English after they move to the United States.

children often learn English in school. Even so, many immigrants to the United States face the challenge of speaking, reading, and writing U.S. English in everyday life.

Most Middle Eastern American immigrants who are children learn English quickly. Some Middle Eastern Americans whose families have lived in the United States for generations no longer speak the languages of their homeland. Others make a point of speaking Arabic or Persian at home. Large Middle Eastern American communities, such as Dearborn, Michigan, offer opportunities to use ancestral languages in public.

The Streets of Dearborn

The Arabic language is a common sight and sound on the streets of Dearborn, Michigan. Dearborn is home to a large Middle Eastern American community. More than thirty thousand people of Middle Eastern heritage live there. That's almost one-third of the city's total population.

Many of Dearborn's Middle Eastern American families arrived in the early 1900s from Lebanon and Syria. Since then Dearborn has attracted more people from other Middle Eastern countries, such as Iraq, Iran, and Yemen.

These stores are part of the Arabian Town Center in Dearborn, Michigan.

This man reads an Iranian newspaper published in Washington, D.C.

EARLY IMMIGRANT LITERATURE

Arabic-speaking Middle Eastern Americans have published Arabic-language newspapers in the United States for more than one hundred years. The earliest U.S. Arabic paper was *Kawkab Amerika* (Star of America). Two brothers of the Syrian Arbeely family of New York City founded this paper in 1892. In 1898 Lebanese immigrant Naoum Mokarzel founded another important Arabic paper, *Al-Hoda* (The Guidance), in Philadelphia, Pennsylvania. In 1902 Mokarzel moved the paper to New York City, where it is still published.

Mokarzel's brother Salloum followed his brother to the United States. He worked for a while at *Al-Hoda*. But soon he realized that many Middle Eastern Americans wanted to read more than news.

They wanted access to literature that addresses their experiences. Salloum Mokarzel founded the *Syrian World* in 1926. This monthly magazine was dedicated to helping the English-speaking Syrian and Lebanese community in the United States. It published plays, stories, poems, and articles in English. Many of its works focused on social issues concerning immigrants and their families. Until its demise in 1932, the *Syrian World* launched many Middle Eastern American literary stars.

Ameen Rihani was one of the best-loved writers published in the *Syrian World*. Rihani was born in Lebanon in 1876. His father was a silk manufacturer. In 1888 Rihani, his father, and his uncle moved to New York City to sell silk. Instead of going to school, Rihani worked in the business. This job helped him perfect his English and gave him time to read great English literature.

By his early twenties, Rihani was writing in both Arabic and English. In 1911 he published *The Book of Khalid*, a novel written in verse (poetry). It was the first English book published by a Middle Eastern American.

For much of his life, Rihani split his time between Lebanon and the United States. He was a popular writer in both countries. He introduced the idea of free verse (poems without regular rhythms and rhymes) to modern Arabic poetry. In the United States, he wrote often about the immigrant experience. In all, he published twenty-nine books in English and twenty-six books in Arabic.

THE PEN LEAGUE

Rihani was just one famous member of the Pen League. This group of Middle Eastern American writers formed in New York in the 1920s. It was also known as Al-Mahjar, or "the immigrant poets."

It included writers from Lebanon and Syria who wrote in Arabic and English. They often wrote about being U.S. immigrants. But they were best known for writing about topics that concern all people, such as the human quest for knowledge and understanding. Some historians say the Pen League created the first widespread interest in U.S. immigrant writers.

Pen League member Gibran Khalil Gibran went on to become one of the best-selling authors in U.S. history. He was born in Lebanon in 1883. In 1895 he moved to Boston, Massachusetts, with his mother and siblings. At the age of fifteen, he went back to Lebanon to attend school. He returned to the United States in 1902.

Lebanese immigrant Gibran Khalil Gibran (1883–1931) was a member of the Pen League.

While Gibran was still in his twenties, he published books in both English and Arabic. Then, in 1923, he published a collection of poems called *The Prophet*. This was the book that launched him to fame.

The Prophet tells of a man who has lived in a foreign city for twelve years and is about to return home. A group of people stops him to discuss various life issues. The book is a collection of twenty-six poetic essays on themes such as religion, love, children, friendship, work, and death. Early critics called it childish. But over many years, it grew popular and sold millions of copies.

Gibran died in 1931. After his death, publishers put out several more of his books. Modern Americans honor him at the Khalil Gibran

Memorial Garden in Washington, D.C., and the Gibran Memorial Plaque at Copley Square in Boston.

Soon after Gibran died, the Pen League faded away. For several decades, few Middle Eastern American writers gained recognition. Then, in the 1980s, Americans showed new interest in Middle Eastern American literature.

MODERN MIDDLE EASTERN AMERICAN WRITERS

Many Middle Eastern Americans have enlivened the U.S. literary scene in the late 1900s and early 2000s. Naomi Shihab Nye is one of them. Nye's father was a Palestinian immigrant, and her mother is German American. Nye lived in Jordan, Israel, and the United States as a child. She eventually settled in Texas and became an acclaimed poet. In addition to poetry, she writes essays and books for young readers. *Sitti's Secrets*, a picture book published in 1994, is one of Nye's most famous children's books. It tells the story of a Palestinian American girl's relationship with her grandmother, who

Author Naomi Shihab Nye speaks to a group of sixth graders at a school in Austin, Texas, in 2007.

still lives in the Middle East. Nye's novel *Habibi* was published in 1997. It tells the story of a Palestinian American teenager who moves with her family to Jerusalem, Israel.

Samuel Hazo is another famous U.S. poet with Middle Eastern roots. His mother was a Lebanese immigrant, and his father was an Assyrian from Jerusalem. (The Assyrian people are an ethnic group living in several Middle Eastern nations.) Hazo has published many volumes of poetry and served as the State Poet of Pennsylvania from 1993 to 2003. Many of his poems deal with universal themes such as suffering or death. He often includes bits of Middle Eastern culture and history. Hazo writes in English and occasionally uses Arabic phrases.

William Peter Blatty, whose parents were from Lebanon, wrote the best-selling 1971 novel *The Exorcist*. Blatty also wrote the screenplay for the 1973 movie based on his novel. The movie became one of the most popular horror films of all time, and Blatty won an Academy Award for the screenplay. He went on to write the novel *The Ninth Configuration*, published in 1978. Two years later, he turned that novel into a movie as well and won Best Screenplay at the 1981 Golden Globe Awards. In all, Blatty has written more than twenty books and screenplays, including the novels *Elsewhere* (2009) and *Dimiter* (2010).

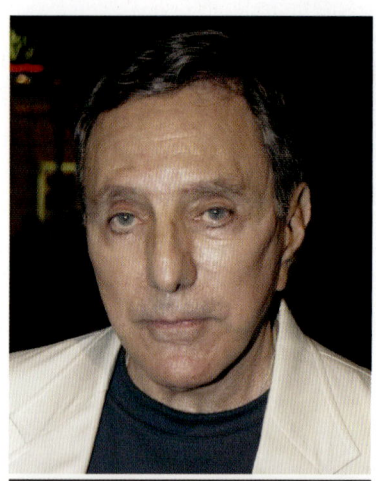

William Peter Blatty wrote the novel *The Exorcist* (1971) and its screenplay (1973).

12 • **THE MIDDLE EASTERN AMERICAN EXPERIENCE**

Elmaz Abinader

Elmaz Abinader *(right)* is a writer whose parents moved to the United States from Lebanon. She grew up in a small Pennsylvania town where most people had European roots. Her schoolmates often teased her because her family was different. They spoke Arabic at home. They ate Lebanese food.

Abinader said she felt like an outcast until she began writing about her Lebanese grandmother in college. About the same time, she read a book by the Chinese American writer Maxine Hong Kingston. Kingston wrote about her Chinese grandmother and about how immigrants often consider their children "too American." Abinader could relate to this book. She began writing more about her experiences as an American child of Middle Eastern immigrants. In 1991 she published her first book, *Children of the Roojme: A Family's Journey from Lebanon*. It tells the story of her family's move to the United States.

Abinader also writes poetry and plays. Her play *Country of Origin* (1997) is about the struggles of three Middle Eastern American women. It includes music that mixes old Middle Eastern sounds and modern jazz.

Mona Simpson is a novelist with an American mother and a Syrian father. She was born in Green Bay, Wisconsin, in 1957. She published her first book, *Anywhere but Here*, in 1986. This story of a stormy mother-daughter relationship was a best-seller and became a movie in 1999. Simpson's novel *Off Keck Road* (2000) was nominated for a PEN/Faulkner Award in 2001. Simpson's husband, Richard Appel, was a writer for the TV show *The Simpsons*. He named one of the show's characters in his wife's honor.

November 11, 2003

From the Pages of USA TODAY
For linguists, job is patriotic duty

For Alex Batlouni and May Kamalick, duty called in the frantic days after the Sept. 11 [2001] terrorist attacks, when FBI Director Robert Mueller pleaded for Americans with foreign-language skills to apply for work as government linguists.

Like many Americans, Batlouni, 45, a manager of a retail store in Las Vegas [Nevada], and Kamalick, 54, a corporate sales trainer in Houston [Texas], wanted to do something to help fight terrorism. But Batlouni figured he was too old to join the military, and Kamalick never imagined that her fluency in Arabic could help the USA in a war.

Mueller's appeal for linguists to help translate hundreds of thousands of documents, audiotapes and videotapes collected here and overseas gave both natives of Lebanon a way to serve the country that took them in 27 years ago.

"It was time to pay back," says Batlouni, who moved his family to Washington, D.C., and took a $55,000-a-year pay cut to work as an FBI language specialist. Kamalick stayed in Houston and accepted an offer from the FBI that paid "pretty close" to what she had made at an insurance company.

Such stories of patriotism and financial sacrifice are common among the hundreds of linguists hired by the FBI since 9/11. But their stories have been overshadowed by the recent arrests of two Defense Department translators at the U.S. military's prison for suspected terror operatives at Guantanamo Bay, Cuba, as part of a probe into suspected spying.

The Guantanamo cases have raised questions about whether the U.S. government is thoroughly screening translators and whether it can hire enough qualified and loyal linguists to decipher evidence in the war on terrorism.

Edward Said was a Palestinian American scholar and author. He was born into an Arab Christian family in Palestine in the 1930s. Palestine then was a mostly Muslim British territory. During Said's childhood, the Jewish nation of Israel was formed in Palestine.

In his adult career, Said drew on his experience growing up as a

14 · THE MIDDLE EASTERN AMERICAN EXPERIENCE

Like the military, the FBI has long relied on private companies to provide translation services. But unlike the military, the FBI has decreased its use of private firms out of fear that the companies aren't thoroughly vetting people who will have access to secret material.

Instead, the FBI is doing its own vetting, hiring linguists directly as contract employees who are paid as much as $38 an hour or as full-time language specialists who earn $33,000 to $78,000 a year.

Overwhelmingly foreign-born, the FBI's linguists have survived a screening process that officials hope is rigorous enough to protect the bureau from scandal. But the background investigations—which can take up to a year—are so demanding that the washout rate for applicants is more than 90%.

From Sept. 17, 2001, when Mueller made his nationwide call for linguists, until Nov. 1, 2001, the FBI received nearly 40,000 applications. Since then, the average has been 1,500 applications a month. The FBI now has 1,198 contract and full-time language specialists, compared with 774 on Sept. 11, 2001. That includes 204 Arabic linguists, compared with 72 on 9/11.

—Toni Locy

Ancient Greek before Arabic?

Enrollment in language programs at four-year U.S. colleges:

Language	Enrollment
Spanish	515,688
French	162,705
German	75,987
Italian	51,750
Japanese	38,545
Latin	27,695
Chinese	26,914
Sign language	21,613
Russian	20,208
Hebrew	16,651
Ancient Greek	14,044
Arabic	8,194

Source: Modern Language Association, 2002 (most recent available)

By Keith Simmons, USA TODAY, 2006

Because so few U.S. students study Arabic, the U.S. government has recruited Arabic-speaking Middle Eastern Americans to help meet its expanding Arabic translation needs.

Christian in tumultuous Israel/Palestine. He became a professor of literature at New York's Columbia University in the 1960s. He gained fame for his 1978 book *Orientalism*, which criticized the biased way in which he believed North American and European scholars study the Middle East.

CHAPTER 2:
MIDDLE EASTERN INFLUENCE ON ART AND MUSIC

Middle Eastern Americans have brought many diverse art forms to U.S. culture. They have contributed unique styles of music, dance, and artistry. And Middle Eastern Americans have also excelled in mainstream U.S. entertainment. They have found fame in pop music, radio, film, and television.

SOUNDS OF THE MIDDLE EAST

The Middle East is home to some of the world's most beautiful music. Middle Eastern Americans have shared many of these sounds in the United States.

For example, classical Arab music has developed over more than one thousand years. It features a wide variety of stringed instruments, such as the oud and the tambura. The oud

The oud is a musical instrument used in classical Arab music.

16 · THE MIDDLE EASTERN AMERICAN EXPERIENCE

resembles a mandolin. It has a short neck and five or six strings. A player plucks the strings. The tambura resembles a lute. It has a long neck and five strings. A player strums the strings.

Israeli music, by contrast, reflects a heavy influence from Germany, France, and other European countries. Many Jewish Israelis emigrated from these countries in the mid-1900s to escape religious persecution and the death camps of Nazi Germany.

Middle Eastern Americans are just as likely to listen to mainstream U.S. music as traditional Middle Eastern music. And some have become popular music stars themselves.

One early pop star, Paul Anka, is Middle Eastern American. His parents emigrated from Lebanon to Canada. Anka became a 1950s teen idol. He topped the charts with songs such as "Lonely Boy," "Put Your Head on My Shoulder" (both in 1959), and "Puppy Love" (1960). After spending most of his career in the United States, Anka became a U.S. citizen in 1990.

In the late 1960s, another Middle Eastern American rose to fame in the music world. Frank Zappa's father was of Arab and Greek descent. (The Arab people are members of several ethnic groups sharing cultural, religious, and language roots of the Arabian Peninsula.) In the late

Singer Paul Anka performs in the 1960s. Anka was a teen idol with fans around the world.

1960s, Zappa and his band the Mothers of Invention became well known for their experimental rock and jazz music. Zappa went on to earn widespread critical acclaim for his songwriting, electric guitar playing, and film directing. He died in 1993.

Gene Simmons, bass player in the 1970s rock band Kiss, was born in Israel. He moved to the United States with his mother when he was eight. Kiss became one of the world's best-selling rock bands in the late 1970s. The band members were famous for wearing face paint, breathing fire, spitting blood, and playing smoking guitars. Gene Simmons remains a rock icon.

Gene Simmons *(center top)* and his Kiss bandmates began playing rock music together in the early 1970s. The band members wore face paint and costumes when performing. Simmons and original member Paul Stanley *(far right)* still tour as Kiss with two new band members.

Hip-hop artist DJ Khaled has Palestinian roots. His birth name is Khaled Khaled. He is a record producer, radio host, and disc jockey for the group Terror Squad. In 2008 he won two Black Entertainment Television (BET) Hip-Hop Awards. He won DJ of the Year and Best Collaboration for the song "I'm So Hood [Remix]" with Young Jeezy, Ludacris, Busta Rhymes, Big Boi, Lil Wayne, Fat Joe, Birdman, and Rick Ross.

DANCE: FROM TRADITIONAL TO POP

Dance was many Americans' introduction to Middle Eastern culture. The earliest known Iranian in the United States was a *semazen* (often called a whirling dervish) who traveled across the country in the 1850s. Semazens are followers of Sufism, or Islamic mysticism. (Mystics follow emotional, intellectual, and physical practices as a path to God.) Semazens spin their bodies while listening to music and meditating. They often wear flowing skirts, which form circles during the dance. The practice is a form of prayer, and it is also an art that requires great skill, focus, and training.

The semazen who visited the United States in the 1850s was known simply as the Traveler. To Americans who had never heard of Sufism, he seemed exotic and mysterious. Word about his striking performances spread before him, and he became a

A semazen performs at a festival in Sacramento, California.

sensation. Some Middle Eastern Americans and others still practice this ritual in the United States. Students can sign up for whirling classes and other Sufi studies at several Sufi retreat centers.

Middle Eastern Americans have brought other dance styles to the United States too. One is *khaleegy*. The word *khaleegy* means "gulf" in Arabic. This women's dance is popular in all the countries near the Persian Gulf. It includes detailed footwork and has a focus on hair. Dancers wear their hair long and flowing and use upper body moves to swirl their hair. Khaleegy is growing popular in the United States both as exercise and as art. Groups such as the Jawaahir Dance Company of Minneapolis, Minnesota, perform a variety of Arab-world dances for diverse audiences and offer classes to the public.

The pop star Paula Abdul got her start in dance. Her father is a Jewish immigrant from Syria. In the mid-1980s, Abdul was a dancer and cheerleader for the Los Angeles Lakers basketball team. She broke into the pop music scene as a choreographer, or someone who arranges dance steps. She went on to release two number-one pop albums. She also scored six number-one singles in the late 1980s and early 1990s. She included some songs with traditional Middle Eastern instruments on her 1995 album *Head over Heels*. She took a break from music in the late 1990s. She returned to the spotlight in 2002 as a judge on the reality TV show *American Idol*.

Singer and dancer Paula Abdul had many hit songs in the late 1980s and early 1990s. She became a judge on the singing contest show *American Idol* in the 2000s.

Actor Jamie Farr, shown here in 1983, starred on the popular television show M*A*S*H in the 1970s and 1980s.

ON SCREEN

Middle Eastern Americans have also succeeded in television and film. In 1972 actor Jamie Farr shot to fame on the hit television show M*A*S*H. The show was about life at a mobile army surgical hospital (MASH) in South Korea during the Korean War (1950–1953). Farr played a soldier who dressed as a woman and acted oddly in an unsuccessful effort to convince his superiors that he was unfit for duty.

In real life, Farr is the son of Lebanese immigrants. He grew up in Toledo, Ohio, and began acting at the age of eleven. His birth name is Jameel Joseph Farah. He changed it to sound more American when he was trying to break into Hollywood in the 1950s. Farr worked in film and TV for many years before finding fame on M*A*S*H. After the show ended in 1983, he continued acting in movies and on television—especially comedies and game shows.

Another famous actor, Tony Shalhoub, is also the son of Lebanese immigrants. Shalhoub got his start playing an Italian cabdriver in the 1990s television show Wings. He went on to star in movies such as Big Night (1996), Men in Black (1997), and Galaxy Quest (1999). From 2002 to 2009, he starred in the TV show Monk.

Shalhoub feels strongly about helping other Middle Eastern Americans break into film. In 2005 he helped start the Arab-American Film Maker Award competition. He did this partly because he thought

MIDDLE EASTERN INFLUENCE ON ART AND MUSIC • 21

November 11, 2003

From the Pages of USA TODAY
Actress is force for change, empowering women

Ask Natalie Portman about her love life, and she'll shut you down. Mention microfinance, and she'll gab for hours.

"People care so much more about who I'm dating," says Portman, who has starred in films from *The Other Boleyn Girl* to *Star Wars*. "We have such an unwarranted spotlight on us."

Diverting attention toward a cause "as opposed to talking about fashion," she says, "is a nice way to dissipate this over interest in people who aren't that interesting."

Anyone who has met Portman knows she's no dummy. The actress, 27, is erudite and thoughtful. In 2003, she graduated from Harvard University with a degree in psychology. That same year, she connected with FINCA International (the Foundation for International Community Assistance), which provides microloans to women in developing countries.

The Israeli-American actress (she was born in Jerusalem) gravitated toward FINCA because of her interest in the Middle East and a desire to collaborate with Jordan's Queen Rania Al-Abdullah, who chairs FINCA's Village Banking campaign.

"She's this incredible woman whom I really admire. She's Palestinian, and I was inspired by her and thought we could do some sort of women's Middle Eastern initiative," Portman says. "When I contacted her office, they said she was really excited about FINCA. I

Hollywood was treating Middle Eastern Americans unfairly. Although U.S. society includes at least one million Middle Eastern Americans, TV shows and movies seldom include Middle Eastern American characters.

After Middle Eastern terrorists hijacked four airliners and killed nearly three thousand people in New York City and near Washington, D.C., on September 11, 2001, Middle Eastern Americans have been

had no idea what that meant, so I started exploring it. And then I started traveling with them to learn about it."

Before affiliating herself with a cause, Portman wanted to learn as much as possible "so I could really stand behind what I am promoting and understand the intricacy of it," she says. "I traveled to Guatemala with (FINCA), and then I went to Uganda and Ecuador and started really learning and seeing, on the ground, how effective the program is. In Guatemala, you don't really see hunger—you see malnourishment. In Uganda, you see real starvation."

You also see progress when struggling women finally acquire things that Americans can buy at Bed Bath & Beyond.

"In Guatemala, I remember seeing a family with four generations of women. It might have even been five. They were together, living together, and the grandmother was watching the baby while the women were in the market," Portman says. "They had a small food stand, and with a loan they were able to buy a scale. That vastly grew their business. They got a refrigerator. Whatever they didn't sell could keep for longer."

Actress Natalie Portman *(left)* with Queen Rania Al-Abdullah of Jordan

Working with FINCA and traveling to developing countries to see its success stories firsthand proved revelatory for Portman.

"It definitely makes you realize how it's really just luck where you're born and what opportunities you're given. It opened my eyes to the fact that we're really the minority in being able to read a newspaper, to be an educated woman who can feed herself," she says.

—Donna Freydkin

subject to stereotyping. Many Americans stereotype Middle Eastern Americans as terrorists. Terrorists are people who use violence to get their way. In the early 2000s, Middle Eastern American film and TV characters are often terrorists or people with bad intentions. Shalhoub and others are trying to get Hollywood to create more ordinary Middle Eastern American characters in movies and TV shows.

Many beautiful carpets come from the Middle East, including these rugs from Turkey.

CRAFT AND VISUAL ARTS

Some traditional Middle Eastern crafts have become popular in the United States. Carpet making, one of the world's oldest art forms, developed in the Middle East about 2000 B.C. People probably first made carpets to cover the earthen floors inside their tents. Historians are not sure who made the world's earliest carpets. But most agree that the craft flourished in Persia (modern Iran). Herds of sheep and goats provided Persian artisans with high-quality wool. For centuries Persians perfected the art of making beautiful rugs. By the late 1800s, local and foreign merchants were exporting great quantities of carpet from Persia to the United States and Europe.

Carpet weaving is the most widespread craft in modern Iran. Persian carpets are famous around the world for their rich colors, intricate patterns, and sturdy construction. After the 1979 Iranian Revolution, many Iranians fled to the United States. (During this violent revolution, an Islamic republic replaced Iran's monarchy, or family of rulers.) Some immigrants managed to bring a few family carpets with them. It is not uncommon to see beautiful Persian carpets in the homes of Iranian Americans.

Americans with Middle Eastern roots have found success in other visual arts, such as painting, photography, and sculpture. Yasser Aggour is an accomplished photographer and painter. He was born in New Jersey to Egyptian parents. He has shown his art widely, including in Los Angeles, California; Paris, France; and New York City. Sabah Al-Dhaher is a well-known sculptor who works in marble, granite, and bluestone. He was born in Iraq and studied classical art there. In 1991 he fled Iraq during the Gulf War. In 1993 he moved to Seattle, Washington. He became well respected in the U.S. art scene by the mid-1990s. In 2003 he created a marble sculpture called *Middle East Peace*, which is on display at the Seattle Center Peace Garden.

Hussam A. Fadhli

Hussam A. Fadhli *(right)* was born in Iraq. As a boy, he had two passionate interests: art and horses. He attended medical school and developed a third passion: medicine. In the 1950s, he immigrated to the United States to practice surgery. He has won great respect as a heart surgeon in Texas. He has also won many awards for his bronze sculptures, most of them depicting horses and people.

MIDDLE EASTERN INFLUENCE ON ART AND MUSIC • 25

Two young men play soccer in Central Park in New York City. Soccer is a popular sport among Middle Eastern Americans to watch and play.

USA TODAY CULTURAL MOSAIC

CHAPTER 3:
EXCELLING IN SPORTS

Sports have always been important in Middle Eastern culture. They include traditional sports such as camel racing and falconry as well as modern sports such as soccer. Many Middle Eastern Americans watch or participate in these sports.

FAVORITE SPORTS

Without a doubt, soccer is the most popular sport in the modern Middle East. Throughout the region, children grow up playing soccer—which most of the world calls football—for everyday recreation. Many children and young adults play in organized leagues as well. And watching professional soccer is a favorite activity for all ages.

All Middle Eastern countries have national soccer teams. They compete internationally in the International Federation of Association Football (better known by its French acronym, FIFA). Middle Eastern American soccer fans often gather to watch matches on television. Many games appear on the Arab Radio and Television (ART) Network. This is a worldwide Arabic-language television station based in Saudi Arabia.

In the countries of Saudi Arabia, Bahrain, Qatar, and the United Arab Emirates, camel racing has been popular for centuries. Many Middle Eastern Americans follow camel racing on cable television.

Camel racing is a lot like horse racing. Its breeding, training, racing, and betting are highly organized. Breeders raise camels to be good racers. Racing camels train on treadmills and in swimming

A robot jockey rides a camel during a race in Dubai in the United Arab Emirates. Many Middle Eastern Americans watch camel racing on television.

pools. Camels can run up to 40 miles (64 kilometers) per hour, so the sport is exciting to watch. Heavy riders slow the camels down, so camel racers prize small riders. Children were once the usual choice for camel jockeys. But child camel jockeys were often ill-treated slaves, and riding a racing camel is dangerous. So several Middle Eastern countries outlawed this practice in the early 2000s. Lightweight robots are replacing child jockeys. The robots guide the camels according to remote-control instructions from their owners on the sidelines.

Horse racing is also popular—both in the Middle East and among Middle Eastern Americans. The Arabian horse, first bred on the Arabian Peninsula, is one of the world's oldest and most desirable racing horse breeds. These horses are famous for their speed, strength, beauty, intelligence, and gentleness. Like camel racing, horse racing is a spectator sport and a betting sport. Many Middle Eastern Americans follow horse racing at racetracks across the United States and on television.

Another traditional Middle Eastern sport is falconry. Falconry is hunting for wild animals using trained falcons or hawks. Falcons and hawks are birds of prey with long wings and hooked claws. People can train these birds to catch small animals and return to their owners with their prey. Historians believe the sport developed at the same time in the Middle East and in northeast Asia as early as 1000 B.C. From these places, it spread around the world. Falconry remains popular in the Middle East. Although it's not as popular in the United States, some hunters do practice it.

MIDDLE EASTERN AMERICAN SPORTS STARS

Many Middle Eastern Americans enjoy playing team sports such as soccer, baseball, football, and basketball. Tennis, swimming, gymnastics, and running are favorite individual sports. Some Middle Eastern Americans have become famous professional athletes.

Doug Flutie is perhaps the biggest Middle Eastern American sports star. He is a Lebanese American football player. He played quarterback for Boston College. In 1984 he won the Heisman Trophy, an award given each year to the best player in U.S. college football. Flutie went on to play professionally for twenty-one years in the U.S. Football League (USFL), National Football League (NFL), and Canadian Football League (CFL). In 2005 he became a TV football announcer. In 2007 he was elected to the College Football Hall of Fame, the Canadian Football Hall of Fame, and the Canadian Sports Hall of Fame. He was the first non-Canadian athlete inducted to the Canadian Sports Hall of Fame.

> Doug Flutie played for many professional football teams in the 1980s, 1990s, and 2000s. In 2005 he became a football announcer for television.

EXCELLING IN SPORTS • 29

Andre Agassi

Emmanuel B. Aghassian was a world-class boxer. He is of Armenian and Assyrian ancestry and was born and raised in Iran. He made the Iranian Olympic team in 1948 and 1952. In the mid-1950s, he moved to the United States and changed his name to Mike Agassi. He lived first in Chicago, Illinois, where he met his wife, Betty, and later in Las Vegas, Nevada.

The Agassis raised four children in Las Vegas. Mike taught them all to play tennis. He drove them hard to be champions. The youngest Agassi child, Andre *(above)*, showed amazing natural talent. When he was thirteen, his parents sent him to train at an elite tennis academy in Florida. Andre Agassi turned professional at the age of sixteen and won his first major tournament at seventeen.

In a career that spanned twenty years, Agassi became one of the greatest tennis players in history. He won sixty tournaments in all, including eight Grand Slam events. Grand Slam tournaments are the most important international tennis events of the year. They include the Australian Open, French Open, U.S. Open, and Wimbledon. Agassi also won a gold medal in the 1996 Olympic Games.

Agassi married the former tennis champion Steffi Graf in 2001. They have two children and live in Las Vegas. Agassi retired from tennis in 2006. In retirement he spends much of his time working with charities to help children. He started the Andre Agassi Charitable Foundation in 1994. This group helps provide educational opportunities for Las Vegas youth. He also started Agassi Prep, a school for disadvantaged teens, in 2001.

Football player Bill George, shown here in 1966, was elected to the Pro Football Hall of Fame in 1974.

Jeff George is another famous pro football quarterback with Lebanese roots. In his sixteen-year career, George played with the Atlanta Falcons, Oakland Raiders, Minnesota Vikings, Washington Redskins, Seattle Seahawks, and Chicago Bears.

Bill George, no relation to Jeff George, was also a Lebanese American football star. He played linebacker for the Chicago Bears from 1952 to 1965. During those years, he played in the Pro Bowl eight times. (The Pro Bowl is an exhibition game played by the best players in the league.) In 1966 he played one year with the Los Angeles Rams. In 1974 he was elected to the Pro Football Hall of Fame.

Major League Baseball, too, has Middle Eastern American stars. Joe Lahoud was a Lebanese American baseball player from 1968 to 1978. He played for the Boston Red Sox, Milwaukee Brewers, California Angels, Texas Rangers, and Kansas City Royals. The first Muslim Middle Eastern American in the major leagues was Sam Khalifa, whose parents emigrated from Egypt. Khalifa played for the Pittsburgh Pirates from 1985 to 1987.

EXCELLING IN SPORTS

Lebanese American Rony Seikaly has made a big name for himself in basketball. Seikaly was born in Lebanon and grew up in Greece. He attended college at Syracuse University in New York and later became a U.S. citizen. He won numerous honors as a center for Syracuse. During this time, he also played for the U.S. national basketball team. He won a gold medal at the International Basketball Federation World Championship in 1986. In 1988 Seikaly joined the National Basketball Association (NBA). In his eleven-season NBA career, he played with the Miami Heat, the Golden State Warriors, the Orlando Magic, and the New Jersey Nets.

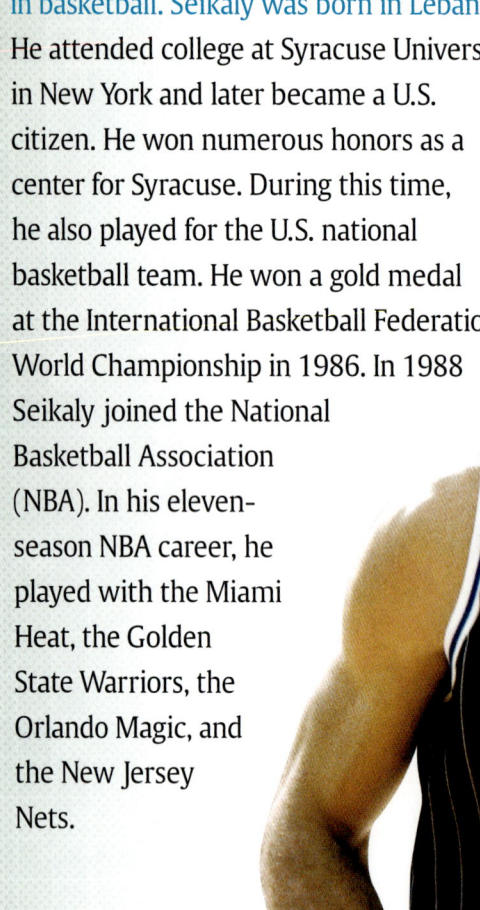

Rony Seikaly played professional basketball for a number of teams in the 1980s and 1990s, including the Orlando Magic. He is shown here playing for the Orlando team in 1997.

This Muslim teenage girl plays soccer while adhering to the modest standard of dress her religion requires.

MIDDLE EASTERN AMERICAN SPORTSWOMEN

Middle Eastern American girls and women are involved in all types of sports. They join school varsity team sports such as basketball and volleyball. They compete in individual sports such as tennis, track, skating, and more.

Middle Eastern American males and females who are observant Muslims or Orthodox Jews are required to dress modestly. For women, this often means covering their arms, legs, and hair in public. Most modern athletic clothing doesn't meet modest standards of dress. For some girls and women, this makes it difficult to participate in sports. But more and more observant females are finding solutions. They may wear longer, looser uniforms when playing team sports. Or they may wear head coverings while practicing sports in public.

EXCELLING IN SPORTS • 33

June 14, 2006

From the Pages of USA TODAY

Some Muslims press public spaces to make room for women's modesty

Muslim women in the USA have been asking the public to accommodate their religious beliefs about modesty, a trend that some Muslims worry will provoke a backlash.

In some recent examples:
- In Lincoln Park, Mich., Fitness USA relented when Muslim women demanded that the gym wall off a co-ed aerobic center from their women-only section because men could see them working out.
- In Bridgeview, Ill., a Muslim school says it wants its girls' basketball team to play road games against non-Muslim schools provided the public schools ban men and teenage boys from the game.
- In North Seattle, Wash., a public pool set up a swim time for Muslim women in which men, even male lifeguards, are banned.

In all of the examples, businesses and public facilities were asked to accommodate followers of one interpretation of Islamic law that says the sexes must be separate if women are not

In the early twenty-first century, no Middle Eastern American women have become famous athletes. This is partly because U.S. society has taken women's athletics seriously only since the 1970s. In addition, most Middle Eastern cultures historically have discouraged females from playing sports. Girls may have felt

34 · THE MIDDLE EASTERN AMERICAN EXPERIENCE

covered with headscarves and modest clothing.

Meeting such demands could create a backlash against Muslims, says Zuhdi Jasser, chairman of American Islamic Forum for Democracy, which advocates separation of religion and government.

"In the long term it does not serve to build friends and bridges with the Western community," says Jasser, a Muslim.

"You're not going to make your American, Christian and Jewish friends feel comfortable... which in the end could create a dislike for Muslims that is unnatural."

But other Muslims see the trend as an issue of civil rights.

Salam Al-Marayati, executive director of Muslim Public Affairs Council, says the right to petition for special accommodation based on religious beliefs is protected by the First Amendment.

"Whether a woman wants to cover her hair or not is her personal choice," he says. "As long as it's not imposed on the rest of society then I don't see any problem."

Walid Phares, a professor of Middle East studies at Florida Atlantic University, sees it as an early sign in the USA of a global Islamic movement to pressure Western society into abiding by Islamic laws.

"These demands exist because there is an ideology of a militant movement to slowly but surely demand more," Phares says. "They will be building on it."

Phares says the conservative Saudi branch of Islam, known as Wahhabism, is trying to assert itself as representing all Muslims in the USA and makes demands most Muslims disagree with.

But Ebrahim Moosa, professor of Islamic studies at Duke University [in Pennsylvania], says the requests are attempts to integrate with U.S. culture. They show "that America can become their home," he says.

—Orin Dorell

cultural pressure against pursuing athletics with the commitment necessary to reach the top ranks. But more and more Middle Eastern American females are joining sports. In the future, U.S. professional sports may well feature more top women athletes with Middle Eastern roots.

CHAPTER 4:
RELIGIOUS FAITHS

Middle Eastern Americans do not share one religion. They may be Christian, Muslim, or Jewish, or they may follow another faith. Christianity, Islam, and Judaism all began in the Middle East. They are called Abrahamic religions because they all trace their ancient roots to one man, Abraham. They have important elements in common. Christianity, Islam, and Judaism are monotheisms. This means they all hold that only one god rules the universe. They view God—or Allah, in Arabic—as the creator of all things and as a holy being who is the source of goodness. They believe God oversees and intervenes in human events.

Almost 90 percent of people living in the modern Middle East

Members of an all-female choir sing at religious services at a Chaldean church in California. The Chaldean Christian Church is based in the Middle East.

36 · THE MIDDLE EASTERN AMERICAN EXPERIENCE

are Muslim. But that doesn't mean most Middle Eastern Americans are Muslim. During the late 1800s and early 1900s, many Christians emigrated from the Middle East to the United States. Many Jews moved in the mid-1900s. In the late 1900s and early 2000s, many Middle Eastern Muslims moved. So the United States is home to large communities of Christian, Jewish, and Muslim Middle Eastern Americans.

MIDDLE EASTERN AMERICAN CHRISTIANS

Christianity has a long history in the Middle East. Its roots, formed in the first century A.D., are in the city of Jerusalem, the capital of modern Israel.

Christians believe that God is one being in three persons. They call this concept the Holy Trinity. The Trinity includes the Father, the Son, and the Holy Spirit. Christians believe that the Son is Jesus of Nazareth, also called Jesus Christ. They believe that Jesus suffered, died, and rose from the dead in Jerusalem. In doing this, he paid for the sins (wrongs) of humankind and opened heaven (eternal life with God) to them.

Christianity was a common religion in the Middle East until the seventh century. In that century, Muhammad, born in 623, founded Islam. Muslim empires began to grow.

Few Christians remain in the modern Middle East. Most of them are members of Eastern Rite churches. This group of churches is related to the Roman Catholic Church. However, they have slightly different beliefs. For instance, rules forbid Roman Catholic priests to marry. But priests in most Eastern Rite churches may marry.

The Maronite Church in Lebanon is an Eastern Rite church. Maronite practices are very similar to Roman Catholic ones.

For example, Maronite priests are not allowed to marry. Almost one-fourth of Lebanon's current population is Maronite.

Maronites have endured many years of persecution. Christians and Muslims who disagreed with Maronite practices or wanted political power over Maronites sometimes treated them harshly.

In the late 1800s, many Maronites moved to the United States to escape this treatment. Most Middle Eastern Americans whose families have lived in the United States for several generations are Maronite Christians from Lebanon. Some Maronite immigrants converted to Roman Catholicism. If they couldn't find a Maronite church, a Roman Catholic Church was the most similar substitute.

In the twenty-first century, dozens of Maronite churches dot the United States. Many are named Our Lady of Lebanon. Some are named after Saint Maron, the founder of the Maronite Church. Other revered Maronite saints, or special holy people, are Saint Anthony, Saint Joseph, and Saint Jude.

Some Middle Eastern Americans are Chaldean Christians. Like the Maronite Church, the Chaldean Christian Church is an Eastern Rite church and is quite similar to Roman Catholicism. Chaldean Christianity developed in the area that became Iraq. About 3 percent of modern Iraqis are Chaldean Christians. Chaldean Christians also live in Iran, Syria, and Turkey. They speak Aramaic, the language Jesus spoke more than two thousand years ago.

Many Chaldean Christians moved to the United States in the early 1900s. Some left their homelands to escape poverty. Others left to escape persecution by Muslims. In the United States, many Chaldean Christians settled near Detroit, Michigan. Jobs in the Ford Motor Company factories attracted them. Nearly eighty thousand Chaldean Americans live in Michigan. Several thousand live in other states too.

Coptic Christians make up one of the largest groups of Christians in the Middle East. About 10 percent of Egyptians are Coptic Christians. They suffer severe discrimination, and many have moved to the United States. Coptic Christian churches have sprung up in many states, especially California, Florida, New Jersey, and New York.

JEWISH REFUGEES

Judaism is the earliest major world religion with origins in the Middle East. Jerusalem is the central holy city to Jews. The religion began nearly four thousand years ago in the region that became Israel. Jews worship the same God that Christians do. (Jesus was a Jew, and Christianity developed upon a foundation of Jewish beliefs and practices.) But Jews do not believe, as Christians do, that Jesus is the Son of God or the Messiah (savior of humankind). Jews believe that they are still waiting for a Messiah. The Jewish concept of the Messiah is a great human leader, such as a king, not a divine (supernatural) savior.

For most of their history, Jews lived throughout the Middle East. Many lived in Syria, Lebanon, Iraq, Yemen, Iran, and Israel. But the powerful Roman Empire (based in Italy) destroyed Jewish rule in Jerusalem in A.D. 70. Afterward, Jews spread to areas around the Mediterranean Sea. By the 700s, Muslims or Christians outnumbered Jews in the Middle East.

In the late 1800s and early 1900s, some people around the globe wanted to create a Jewish nation in the Jews' ancient homeland of Palestine (a region that lies roughly between the Mediterranean Sea and the Jordan River valley). Jews had suffered persecution all around the world for centuries, especially from European Christians. They wanted a safe homeland. During World War II (1939–1945), the Nazi regime in Germany murdered six million Jews. Afterward, the state

Young people attend services at a Jewish synagogue (house of worship) in California.

of Israel was born in 1948. Hundreds of thousands of Jews moved there from elsewhere in the Middle East and from Europe. The creation of Israel took land from the citizens of Palestine, most of whom were Arab Muslims. The loss of this land and the flood of Jewish immigrants angered other Arab nations and sparked the Arab-Israeli War of 1948–1949.

After Israel won the war, most Middle Eastern countries expelled (kicked out) their Jewish citizens. Jews from groups native to the Middle East are called Mizrachi Jews. Some Mizrachi refugees moved to Europe or the Americas. Most moved to Israel. But even in Israel, Mizrachi Jews sometimes faced discrimination from European Jews. So many Mizrachi eventually emigrated from Israel to the United States. An estimated two hundred thousand to three hundred thousand Mizrachi Jews live in the United States in the twenty-first century.

Some second- and third-generation European Jews have also emigrated from Israel to the United States. Many Jews leave Israel to escape the ongoing violence between Muslims and Jews there. Some move to join family members in the United States. And others travel— either temporarily or permanently—for jobs or education.

Jewish immigrants from the Middle East often settle in cities that have large, established Jewish communities, such as New York City and Los Angeles. Jewish immigrants to these areas can easily find a place of worship. They also find a community with familiar beliefs and customs.

FOLLOWERS OF ISLAM

The most common religion in the modern Middle East is Islam. Islam is the world's second-largest religion after Christianity. Like Christianity and Judaism, Islam originated in the Middle East and views Jerusalem as a holy city.

Muslims believe in the same God that Christians and Jews do. Muslims call this god Allah. The word *Islam* means "surrender to the will of Allah."

Muslims believe Allah spoke directly to his prophet (spiritual spokesperson) Muhammad through the angel Gabriel in the A.D. 600s. Allah revealed to Muhammad how people should live together and how they should worship. Allah said that Christians and Jews had lost their way. Muslims believe that the holy scriptures of the Quran are the actual words of God, as revealed to Muhammad. Muslims try to fulfill Allah's wishes as expressed in the Quran. They also look to

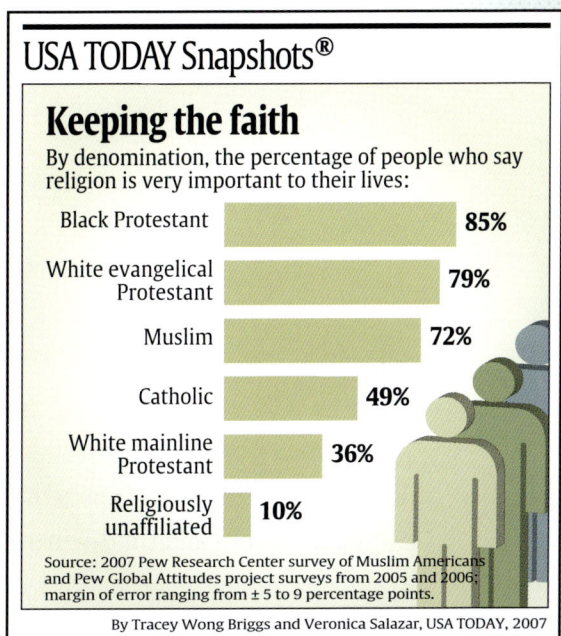

USA TODAY Snapshots®

Keeping the faith
By denomination, the percentage of people who say religion is very important to their lives:

Denomination	Percentage
Black Protestant	85%
White evangelical Protestant	79%
Muslim	72%
Catholic	49%
White mainline Protestant	36%
Religiously unaffiliated	10%

Source: 2007 Pew Research Center survey of Muslim Americans and Pew Global Attitudes project surveys from 2005 and 2006; margin of error ranging from ± 5 to 9 percentage points.

By Tracey Wong Briggs and Veronica Salazar, USA TODAY, 2007

Muslims are among the most devout Americans. Nearly three-quarters of Muslim Americans say Islam plays a key role in their lives.

RELIGIOUS FAITHS • 41

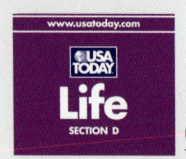

October 3, 2006

From the Pages of USA TODAY

Rapping in the name of interfaith tolerance; Muslims, Jews strive to increase the peace

Chicago actor and musician Yuri Lane mixes prayers for Middle Eastern peace into his rap verses.

The Jewish artist has brought his play *From Tel Aviv to Ramallah* to college campuses, community centers and theaters across the country. In collaboration with Egyptian-American DJ Sharif Ezzat, Lane uses "beatbox" music, created by his lips, hands, teeth and diaphragm, to portray an Israeli and a Palestinian who face off at a checkpoint between their homelands.

"My show is a modern retelling of Isaac and Ishmael," says Lane, 35, invoking the biblical story of the two sons of Abraham. One of the half-brothers became a patriarch of the Jews, the other an ancestor claimed by Muslims.

"I wish they could get together," he adds wistfully.

Maybe they can. As the Jewish holidays of Rosh Hashanah and Yom Kippur intersect with the Muslim holy month of Ramadan this year, interfaith rappers are joining forces to teach their audiences a lesson about peace.

Lane, whose album *Yuri Lane: Hu-*

Muhammad's example as recorded in the hadith—the collection of Muhammad's words and deeds.

The central idea of Islam is that one god, Allah, is the all-knowing creator of the universe. Islam also emphasizes people's responsibility to their communities. Muslims follow rules about their diet and how they live together. For example, Muslims may not eat pork or drink alcohol. Islam encourages men and women to wear modest clothing in public.

man *Beatbox* will be released Nov. 1, joined Jewish and Arab rappers in New York City last month for a concert dubbed "Hip-Hop Sulha," an Arabic term for peaceful negotiation.

Some of the performers, including Omar Chakaki, the Syrian-American lead singer for a group called the N.O.M.A.D.S, say they were inspired to rap by the Sept. 11 terrorist attacks.

The musicians disagree over the precise solution for the Arab-Israeli conflict and favor either a single secular government, a two-state solution or a demilitarized semi-autonomous Palestine.

But all agree that music can help stop the bloodshed.

Nizar Wattad, 25, the Palestinian-American lead singer of The Philistines, once taught hip-hop in refugee camps in the West Bank.

"I worked with children who watched one of their friends get shot at a checkpoint," says Wattad, whose stage name is Ragtop.

"I helped them adapt their story into a rap verse, taught them to sample, create musical loops and record their own voices. It gave them creative alternatives to throwing rocks at soldiers."

Hasidic Jewish rapper Yitzchak Jordan, 28, who calls himself Y-love, combines Arabic lyrics with his English, Hebrew and Yiddish rhymes on his upcoming album *This Is Babylon*, scheduled for release in the spring. Jordan, who also has read the Quran, believes that greater education in religious writings will help bring understanding. In his song "6000," he criticizes religious and political leaders who preach intolerance.

Palestinian singer Sameh Zakout, 23, known as Saz, who was raised in the Israeli city of Ramle, near Tel Aviv, also uses music as a non-violent means of protest.

"I don't see my Palestine being built by blood," says Zakout, who will tour in France in October to publicize his album *Min Yum*. "It should be built by negotiations, not bombings in Tel Aviv. My bullets are my rhymes. My M-16 [rifle] is my microphone."

—*Rachel Breitman*

Muslims around the world strive to fulfill five central duties. These are called the five pillars of Islam. They include declaring faith in Allah as the one god and in Muhammad as his prophet; praying five times daily; fasting from sunrise to sunset during the holy month of Ramadan; giving charity; and traveling to the holy city of Mecca, Saudi Arabia, once in a lifetime if possible. Friday is the day of group worship for Muslims.

The U.S. Muslim population is growing rapidly. Much of this

Muslim American women pray during a meeting in New York City in 2006.

growth is due to immigration by Middle Eastern Muslims. Many move to the United States for school or jobs. In the early and mid 1900s, Muslims who came to the United States for an education often returned home once they finished school. One key reason was the difficulty of practicing Islam in the United States at that time. Muslim Americans were few, mosques (Islamic houses of worship) were hard to find, and most Americans understood little about Islam.

In the late 1900s and early 2000s, the U.S. Muslim population is much larger. Many U.S. cities have mosques. Americans are becoming more accepting of practices of Muslims, such as taking breaks to pray. Most Muslim Americans live in four parts of the United States. One is the triangle region between Chicago, Cleveland, and Detroit. Another is Texas—especially the Houston and Dallas–Fort Worth areas. The other two are the cities of Los Angeles and San Francisco in California.

Anti-Muslim Discrimination

Many Muslim Americans face discrimination because their practices stand out in U.S. society. Since September 11, 2001, when a group of radical Middle Eastern Muslim terrorists carried out deadly attacks in the United States, Muslim Americans have faced even greater discrimination.

Some terrorists are radical Muslims. They believe that they will achieve a perfect Islamic world through violence. Mainstream Muslims do not support violence. U.S. Muslims have spoken out against terrorism. They have explained that radicals and terrorists do not represent their views. However, some non-Muslim Americans continue to treat Muslim Americans unfairly.

This discrimination has made life difficult for many Muslim Americans. Some say they feel like criminals. Others are uncomfortable practicing their faith. Some mosques have suffered vandalism. In several cases, strangers have physically attacked or threatened the lives of Muslims in the United States. Muslim Americans find they must work very hard to earn fair treatment in many parts of the nation. Many have trouble finding jobs or housing.

Muslims in America
Views on life here:
- Muslim Americans
- General public

Believe you can get ahead with hard work
- 71%
- 64%

Rate your community as excellent or good
- 72%
- 82%

Satisfied with the state of the United States
- 38%
- 32%

Source: Pew Research Center Poll of 1,050 Muslim American adults Jan. 24–April 30. Margin of error is ± 5 percentage points. General public data taken from surveys conducted in October 2005, March 2006, January and February.

USA TODAY, 2007

Despite anti-Muslim discrimination, Muslim Americans hold generally positive views of life in the United States. Their rate of satisfaction is similar to that of the general U.S. public.

Dancers participate in the New York Persian Day Parade in 2009. The parade celebrates Nauruz, the Iranian New Year.

USA TODAY CULTURAL MOSAIC

CHAPTER 5:
CELEBRATING HOLIDAYS

The table is loaded with food. A large platter of turkey takes center stage. Steaming bowls of stuffing and mashed potatoes flank the turkey. So do a big dish of hummus (chickpea dip) and a pot of okra-and-lamb stew. Welcome to a Lebanese American Thanksgiving.

Most Middle Eastern Americans celebrate the same secular (nonreligious) holidays other Americans do. Often they add Middle Eastern touches. They might serve lamb stew at Thanksgiving or stuffed grape leaves at a Fourth of July picnic.

KEEPING FAMILY CLOSE

One key aspect of most Middle Eastern American celebrations is the family group. Middle Eastern American families are not necessarily large, but family relationships are very important.

In Middle Eastern countries, extended families often live together. (An extended family includes not just parents and their children but also relatives such as grandparents, aunts, uncles, and cousins.) This practice isn't as common among Middle Eastern Americans, but extended families do tend to remain close.

A Middle Eastern American hosting a celebration typically invites parents, siblings, grandparents, aunts, uncles, and cousins. When grown children live far from their parents, they usually travel home for big holidays.

Middle Eastern immigrants who don't have family in the United States often form a tight-knit social group with other immigrants.

Nauruz

Many Iranian Americans celebrate Nauruz, the Iranian New Year. The Persian word *nauruz* means "new day." The holiday marks the arrival of spring. Iranian Americans may practice some traditional customs on this day. Families have large parties, and children often receive presents. The centerpiece of the day is the *haft sin* (seven *S*s) table. This is a display of seven objects whose names begin with the letter *S* in Persian and carry a symbolic meaning. They are greens, apples, and Russian olives for abundance; gold coins for wealth; hyacinth for beauty; and vinegar and garlic to represent life's bitter times.

This group may celebrate religious holidays, birthdays, and other occasions together. Children of recent immigrants sometimes call their parents' friends "aunt" or "uncle." In this way, immigrants rebuild their extended families.

CELEBRATING ISLAM

Only about one-third of Middle Eastern Americans are Muslim. But the overall U.S. Muslim population is growing. As a result, U.S. society is growing more familiar with major Islamic holidays. Muslim Americans with roots in Africa, Asia, and the Middle East often celebrate major holidays together.

The month of Ramadan on the Islamic calendar is a holy month for all Muslims. The Islamic calendar is different from the U.S. calendar. They both have twelve months. But the U.S. calendar is based on the sun, and most of its months are thirty or thirty-one days long. The Islamic

48 · THE MIDDLE EASTERN AMERICAN EXPERIENCE

calendar is based on the moon, and each of its months is only twenty-nine or thirty days long. Ramadan is the ninth month. It is the month when Allah first revealed the words of the Quran to Muhammad.

To show their devotion to Allah, Muslims fast for the month of Ramadan. They do not eat or drink from dawn to sunset. Muslims fast partly to experience hunger and remember the importance of helping the poor. Fasting also builds self-control. It is a way for Muslims to practice putting others' needs before their own.

During Ramadan, Muslims focus on prayer and charity. Some Muslims read the entire Quran. In countries with large Muslim populations in the Middle East, businesses and governments shut down fully or partially for most of Ramadan. But in the United States, few Muslims can take a month off from their jobs.

The first day of the month following Ramadan is a special holiday. This is the day that Muslims break their fast. It's called Eid al-Fitr,

Worshippers read from the Quran during Ramadan services in California.

Gathering for Celebration

Many Muslim Americans attend community celebrations for Eid al-Fitr and Eid al-Adha. Such festivals often take place in large cities, such as Orlando, Florida; Washington, D.C.; Los Angeles; and Chicago. Muslim community celebrations resemble multicultural carnivals. Vendors sell books and clothing from around the Muslim world. Kids can enjoy rides or play carnival games. Abundant food stalls sell specialties from the Middle East, Asia, and Africa.

which means the Festival of the Breaking of the Fast. Most Muslim Americans begin this day by attending a prayer service at a mosque. Then they visit relatives and begin a day of feasting and celebration. Children often receive gifts of money, new clothes, or small toys. Middle Eastern Americans with relatives in other countries often telephone their relatives.

The Eid al-Fitr menu depends on a family's heritage. For example, families from Iraq often have a lamb dish. Then they may have a date-filled pastry called *klaicha*. Palestinian Americans make a pastry called *k'ak al-tamar* that's filled with dried fruit and nuts. Giving to the poor is just as important as feasting on Eid al-Fitr. Muslims always give *zakat* (charitable donations) to mark the end of Ramadan.

After Ramadan and Eid al-Fitr, the most important Muslim holiday is Eid al-Adha. Its name means Festival of the Sacrifice. This holiday honors Abraham's willingness to sacrifice his son to

Allah. The story of Abraham's devotion to God is part of Jewish and Christian tradition too. The Muslim festival always takes place in the tenth day of the twelfth month on the Islamic calendar. This is also the time of an annual mass pilgrimage of Muslims to Mecca.

In the Middle East, families sacrifice an animal on Eid al-Adha if they can afford to do so. The animal is usually a sheep, goat, camel, or cow. They slaughter the animal in a religious ceremony and then divide the meat among themselves, friends and neighbors, and the poor. In the United States, some Muslims buy meat from specially chosen, ritually slaughtered animals. Most Muslims mark the day by attending prayer services and then feasting with family and friends.

Islamic Funerals

Many Middle Eastern American Muslims practice Islamic funeral customs. They bathe a body three times, the last time with scented oil. They say special prayers during the bathing. Then they wrap the body in a white shroud (burial garment). If a person died in the morning, burial must happen that day. If a person died in the afternoon, burial must occur by the following morning. During the burial ceremony, family and friends recite prayers. The body must lie on its right side, facing Mecca. Coffins are allowed but are not common. Tombs and lavish headstones are forbidden.

CELEBRATING JUDAISM

Middle Eastern American Jews celebrate Jewish holidays along with other U.S. Jews. The Jewish calendar includes twelve main holidays. The ones U.S. Jews most commonly observe are Rosh Hashanah, Yom Kippur, Hanukkah, and Passover. All Jewish holidays begin at sunset on the preceding evening.

The two most important Jewish holidays are Rosh Hashanah and Yom Kippur. Rosh Hashanah is the Jewish New Year, and it falls in September or October. On Rosh Hashanah, Jews look back on the old year and promise to do better in the new year. It is a happy, festive holiday. In Jewish communities in the Middle East, schools and businesses are closed on Rosh Hashanah. In the United States, many Jews stay home from work or school and go to worship services.

Ten days after Rosh Hashanah is the holiday of Yom Kippur, or the Day of Atonement. On this day, Jews fast to repent (express regret) for the mistakes they made the previous year. Many Middle Eastern American Jews have a large family meal on the evening before Yom Kippur. The next day, they stay home from work or school and go to worship services.

Hanukkah is an eight-day holiday that falls between Thanksgiving and Christmas. It commemorates an event that happened in Jerusalem in the 100s B.C. The Jews had just won a battle against the Greeks. But the Greeks had desecrated (contaminated) the Jewish temple. To reconsecrate the temple (rededicate or make it holy again), the Jews needed to keep its eternal light lit. But they had only enough oil to burn for one day. Somehow the oil lasted for eight days—long enough to prepare more consecrated olive oil.

In the Middle East, Jewish families gather each evening of Hanukkah to light candles on an eight-branched menorah. They light one candle the first night, two the second night, and so on. They do not celebrate Hanukkah much more than that.

In the United States, Jews often celebrate Hanukkah with gift giving and special meals. This difference is due to the holiday's nearness to Christmas. With so many U.S. festivities celebrating Christmas, some Jewish Americans decide to counterbalance Christmas with Hanukkah. Large Hanukkah decorations and parties are common. The menu always includes some food fried in oil to honor the miracle of the oil, such as *livivot* (potato pancakes) and *sufganiyot* (doughnuts). Parents may give gifts to their children on each of the holiday's eight nights. But gathering with family to light the menorah remains the key activity.

Passover is another holiday central to Judaism. It recalls the story of the Exodus, the Jews' escape from slavery in ancient Egypt, led by Moses. Passover lasts eight days and occurs in March or April. Middle Eastern American Jews usually hold a ritual dinner called a seder on the first night of Passover. Seder foods include lamb, bread without yeast, bitter herbs, and wine. Each of these foods symbolizes part of the Exodus story. Jews with Middle Eastern roots might add traditional Middle Eastern touches to the seder, such as a lamb-and-tomato stew or dried fruits and nuts.

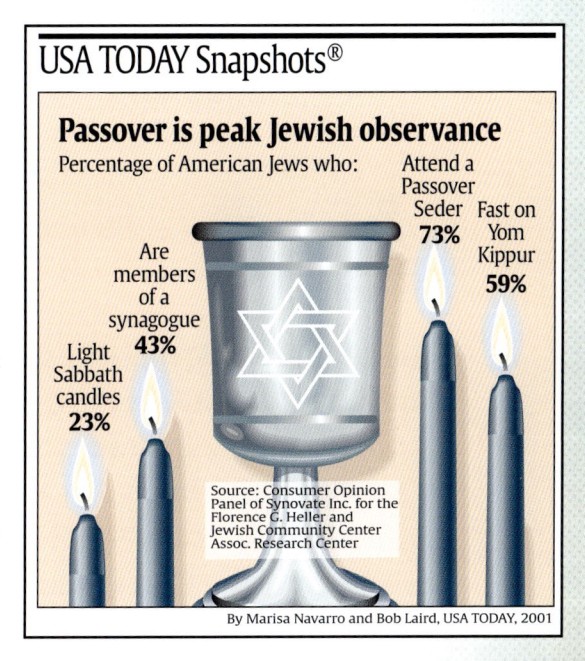

USA TODAY Snapshots®

Passover is peak Jewish observance
Percentage of American Jews who:

- Attend a Passover Seder **73%**
- Fast on Yom Kippur **59%**
- Are members of a synagogue **43%**
- Light Sabbath candles **23%**

Source: Consumer Opinion Panel of Synovate Inc. for the Florence G. Heller and Jewish Community Center Assoc. Research Center

By Marisa Navarro and Bob Laird, USA TODAY, 2001

From the Pages of USA TODAY

Unwrapping spirit of Hanukkah: Giving to charity

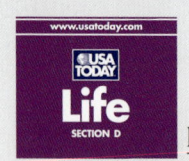

December 4, 2007

When Jews light the first candle in their Hanukkah menorahs tonight, many join a modern trend of nightly gift-giving that rivals Christmas for consumer largesse [generosity].

But some will receive one box that needs no unwrapping: a tzedakah box, used to collect coins for a good cause. Tzedakah (tseh-DUH-kuh) is Hebrew for charity, a righteous obligation in Judaism.

Like many Christians who want to see Christ, not toys, emphasized at Christmas, many Jewish families are highlighting the spiritual side of Hanukkah by devoting at least one of the holiday's eight nights to tzedakah, says parenting writer Sharon Duke Estroff.

"It's a time of year when kids lose perspective, and they have a real sense of entitlement.... Tzedakah is a balancer. When you add a tzedakah box or a day of service to the holiday celebration mix—something that should be built into what Jews do in life—kids love it," says Estroff, an Atlanta mother of four and author of *Can I Have a Cell Phone for Hanukkah? The Essential Scoop on Raising Modern Jewish Kids.*

"Since children are seen as part of the whole community, they, too, are encouraged to participate in living the Jewish teaching of tzedakah," says Vivian Mann, professor of Jewish art history at the Jewish Theological Seminary in New York.

Although Hanukkah dates to 165 B.C., the phenomenon of tzedakah box-

CELEBRATING EASTERN RITE CHRISTIANITY

Most Middle Eastern American Christians celebrate religious holidays alongside other U.S. Christians. Christmas is often the biggest holiday of the year. This day marks the birth of Jesus.

Many Middle Eastern American Christians celebrate Christmas with the traditions of Santa Claus, decorated Christmas trees, and lots

es, as humble as cardboard or tin or as elegant as sterling silver, began in the 19th century.

Jewish institutions sent out little boxes emblazoned with symbols of their synagogue, school or orphanage. People would donate on the Sabbath, on holy days and in honor of life cycle events, says Mann, whose grandmother had a collection of seven or eight boxes.

The best-known tzedakah boxes are the little blue boxes sent out by the Jewish National Fund since 1901. The proceeds went to buy land in the Holy Land, "long before Israel was established or anyone knew what its borders might be," says fund CEO Russell Robinson. Just $1 million of the $60 million the fund raised last year to support development and forests in Israel came from the blue boxes. But the group still sends out 150,000 a year on request.

Many of those who write the big checks learned the habit of giving with coins as children, Robinson says. "It teaches the history of our people, the importance of responsibility for all."

Indeed, sales of tzedakah boxes were up 25% in 2006, says Debbie Dorfman, director of new business development for the two Judaica [Jewish cultural and religious items] shops at the Jewish Museum in Manhattan [New York].

It's not only parents who are making the purchases. Jewish institutions are using them for gifts to honor volunteers and new graduates. Tzedakah boxes are a popular wedding gift as well because they're "considered part of establishing a Jewish household," Dorfman says.

—Cathy Lynn Grossman

This tzedakah box is titled *Joy*. New Mexico artist Alice Warder Seely made it.

of presents. But others, especially those who live in tight-knit Middle Eastern American communities, hold on to traditions from their home countries. For example, some Lebanese families sprout small seeds in damp cotton balls about two weeks before Christmas. The seeds are usually chickpeas, lentils, or other beans. Once the sprouts grow about 6 inches (15 centimeters), people place them around the manger in a Nativity scene. A Nativity scene is a display depicting the setting of Jesus's birth.

For some Middle Eastern American Christians, Easter is a bigger holiday than Christmas. Christians around the world celebrate Jesus's resurrection from the dead on this day. Eastern Rite churches follow a different religious calendar than most U.S. churches do. So sometimes Middle Eastern Americans celebrate Easter on a different day than other U.S. Christians.

Many Lebanese American families begin their celebration the night before Easter. They boil eggs with onion skins to turn the eggshells reddish brown. For dinner that night, they eat the eggs along

Eastern Rite Christians celebrate Easter with a meal after services in New York City. The participants are breaking Easter eggs dyed red as part of a holiday tradition.

Saint Barbara's Day

Some Middle Eastern American Christians celebrate Saint Barbara's Day on December 4. Saint Barbara is the patron saint of miners, firefighters, and others who work with explosives and fire, because lightning features prominently in her story.

According to legend, Saint Barbara converted to Christianity against her father's wishes. Her father locked her in a tower. Later, he killed her. And when she died, lightning struck her father and turned him into a pile of ashes.

In the Middle East, children dress in costumes and collect treats on Saint Barbara's Day. Some Middle Eastern Americans celebrate this holiday in a similar way. A popular dish served on Saint Barbara's Day is *burbara*. Burbara is Arabic for Barbara. It is also a pudding made from wheat and apricots.

with breads and sweet pastries. The next morning, children rush to whisper to their parents, "The Lord is risen!" According to tradition, the first person to whisper this phrase gets a gift of coins. On Easter morning, cracked eggs symbolize Jesus rising from the dead.

This Lebanese meal includes a green bean stew with lamb, a bowl of rice, and a sesame dip.

USA TODAY CULTURAL MOSAIC

CHAPTER 6:
TASTES OF THE MIDDLE EAST

Most Middle Eastern American families eat a variety of foods from around the world. They may eat Italian pasta one day, Mexican fajitas the next, and Japanese sushi the next. But in some families, meals are a way to preserve their cultural heritage.

This chapter takes a look at some common recipes and food customs of the two largest groups of Middle Eastern Americans, Lebanese Americans and Iranian Americans. The cuisines of Lebanon and Iran represent many of the flavors and cooking styles popular throughout the Middle East. Middle Eastern Americans from all backgrounds are likely to be familiar with foods like those described below.

LEBANESE AMERICAN FLAVOR

Many Lebanese American families have lived in the United States for three or more generations. Families who arrived in the early 1900s often tried hard to assimilate (fit in) with their new culture. In general, most made an effort to dress, talk, and eat like other Americans. Therefore, long-established Lebanese American families may not eat much Lebanese cuisine regularly.

However, traditional foods are a big source of comfort and pride for immigrants. Many Lebanese American families do continue to cook and eat Lebanese style, at least on some occasions. Lamb is a main ingredient in many Lebanese dishes. Ground lamb mixed with bulgur (cracked wheat) is called kibbe. Ground lamb mixed

Stuffed grape leaves are a popular dish in Middle Eastern cooking.

with rice is called *mahshee*. Lebanese cooks may stuff mahshee into grape leaves and eat them with yogurt or into cabbage leaves and eat them with lemon juice. Another popular way to serve mahshee is in a dish called *kousa mahshee*. A cook scoops out the insides of summer squash (such as a zucchini), stuffs mahshee into the squash, and cooks the squash with tomato sauce.

Several Lebanese foods popular throughout the Middle East are common in the United States. Pita bread, hummus, baba ghanoush (eggplant dip), and tabbouleh (a salad of parsley, bulgur, onions, mint,

Middle Eastern Treats

Many Middle Eastern desserts feature nuts, honey, and dried fruits, such as dates. Some of the most popular are:

baklava (above): phyllo layered with honey or syrup and chopped nuts
esh asaraya: a sweet cheesecake topped with cream
mehalabiya: pudding sprinkled with rose water and pistachio nuts
umm ali: a type of bread pudding

lemon juice, olive oil, and tomatoes) often show up on U.S. restaurant menus and in grocery stores. Baklava is a popular Middle Eastern dessert in the United States. It is made of finely chopped nuts and honey or syrup between layers of phyllo dough (paper-thin pastry).

EATING THE IRANIAN WAY

A traditional Iranian meal often includes rice and a stew made from lamb, chicken, or beans. Or it might feature pan-fried fish or chicken. Most meals also include yogurt and fruits and vegetables. Grapes, melons, tomatoes, and cucumbers are all popular.

Some of the earliest Iranian immigrants to the Unites States found it hard to prepare the foods they were used to eating. They couldn't find the variety of rice or the spices common in Iran. But after the Iranian Revolution, many more Iranians moved to the United States. They formed Iranian American communities such as Little Tehran in Los Angeles. (Tehran is the capital of Iran.) Iranians opened specialty grocery stores in their communities. Meanwhile, more U.S. grocery chains began carrying a wider variety of ethnic foods. In the twenty-first century, Iranian Americans can easily prepare most Iranian foods.

Tea drinking plays a major role in Iranian culture. Hosts always offer *chaay* (tea) to visitors in their homes. Iranians serve

This Iranian dish includes spicy beef and cherries in a bowl of rice.

TASTES OF THE MIDDLE EAST • 61

Common Middle Eastern Dishes

The following dishes are common throughout the Middle East. They are also common in Middle Eastern American restaurants and homes.

arayes kofta: bread with grilled lamb
baba ghanoush: broiled eggplant blended with tahini (a paste of ground sesame seeds), lemon juice, and olive oil
falafel: a fried patty or ball made of ground, seasoned chickpeas
fatteh: a baked chickpea and pita dish served with a type of yogurt called *leben*
fattoush: salad of greens and vegetables topped with toasted or fried pita pieces and a tangy lemon dressing
khoshkash kabob: skewered meat in a spicy tomato sauce
shish tawook: marinated chicken grilled on skewers

tea very hot. Often they pour a small amount in their saucer to cool before they drink it. In communities such as Little Tehran, Iranian Americans gather in teahouses to meet friends, drink tea, and listen to music or poetry.

Drinking tea is popular in Iran and throughout the Middle East. This is a traditional Iranian teapot.

Falafel

Falafel is a popular fast food in the Middle East. Middle Eastern Americans eat falafel as a sandwich, stuffed in pita bread with lettuce, tomatoes, and tahini.

INGREDIENTS

1 15-ounce can chickpeas, drained
½ large onion, roughly chopped (about 1 cup)
2 tablespoons finely chopped fresh parsley
2 tablespoons finely chopped fresh cilantro
1 teaspoon salt
½ to 1 teaspoon dried hot red pepper
4 cloves garlic
1 teaspoon cumin
1 teaspoon baking powder
4 to 6 tablespoons flour
vegetable oil for frying

PREPARATION

1. Place the chickpeas and 1 cup chopped onions in the bowl of a food processor fitted with a steel blade. Add the parsley, cilantro, salt, hot pepper, garlic, and cumin. Process until blended but not pureed.
2. Sprinkle in the baking powder and 4 tablespoons of the flour, and pulse the food processor. Add enough flour so the dough forms a small ball and doesn't stick to your hands. Turn dough ball into a bowl and refrigerate, covered, for several hours.
3. Form the dough into balls about the size of walnuts.
4. Ask an adult to help you heat 3 inches of oil to 375°F in a deep pot or wok, and fry one ball to test. If it falls apart, add a little flour to the dough. Then fry about six balls at once for a few minutes on each side, or until golden brown. Drain on paper towels.

DIETARY LAWS AND CUSTOMS

For the many Middle Eastern Americans who are Muslim or Jewish, some food customs are more than just traditions. They are religious requirements.

The Quran includes rules governing foods and preparation methods that are halal (permitted) and haram (forbidden). The main purpose of these rules is to help Muslims avoid eating anything considered unclean by Allah. For instance, eating pork is forbidden. So is eating any type of meat-eating animal or bird, such as lions, wolves, vultures, or eagles. Muslims are also forbidden to drink alcohol or use any mind-altering drugs, except those that are medically necessary.

Islamic law also describes specific ways to slaughter animals. Muslims must kill livestock quickly in a way that causes as little pain

Common Sense and Dietary Laws

Many Islamic and Jewish food restrictions probably sprang from health concerns. For instance, the disease trichinosis is caused by worms that can live in pigs' intestines and muscles. Long ago, when food safety was not well understood, trichinosis was a grave threat to humans. And without modern medicine, people who caught this disease often died. Avoiding pork was a smart move for everyone. That religious leaders encouraged this food restriction makes sense.

Islamic and Jewish dietary laws also forbid eating any animal that died due to natural causes, such as illness. This too is a good health practice. Eating animals that may be diseased is not wise for anyone.

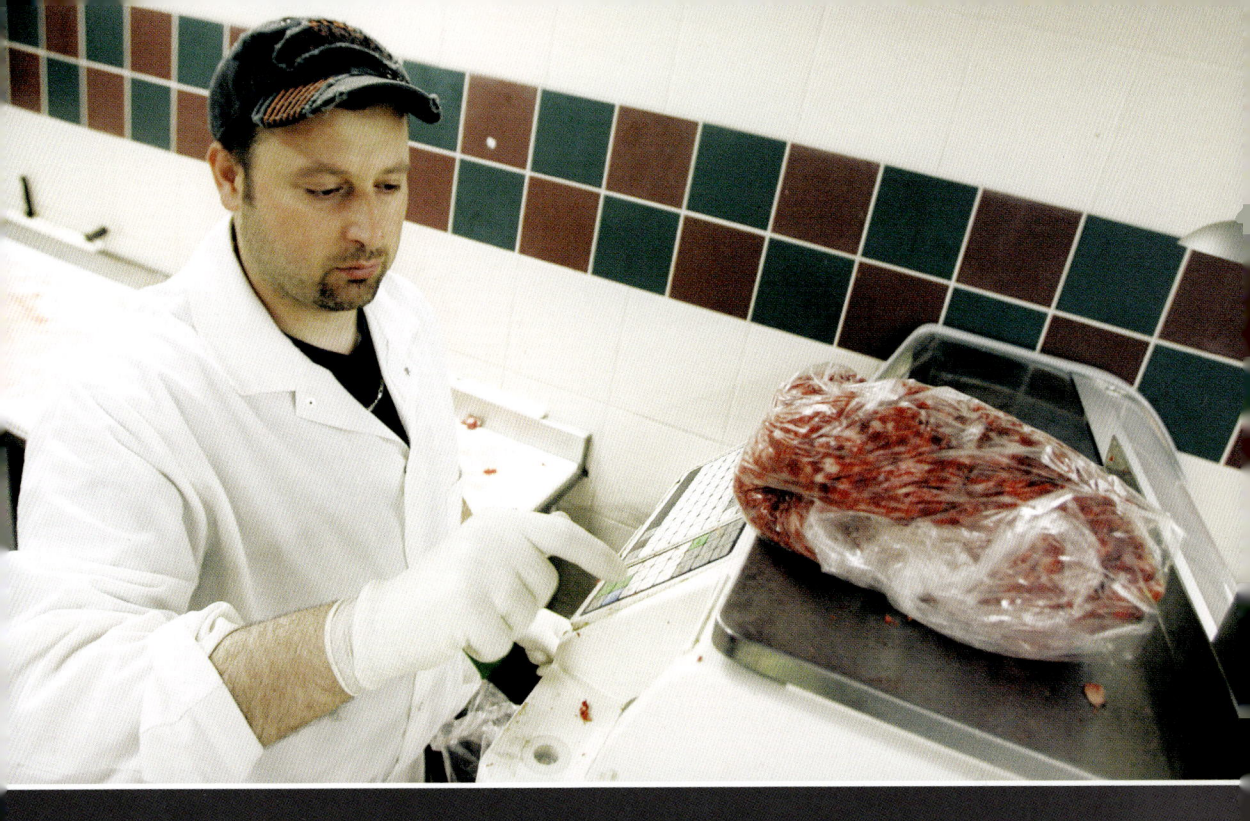

Butcher Nehme Mansour weighs halal meat at a grocery store in Dearborn, Michigan. The store is one of only a few in the country that are halal certified. Kosher certifications are more common in the United States.

as possible. They must also say a prayer of thanks to Allah at the time of slaughter. Muslims cannot eat animals that have died in other ways.

Jewish dietary law is called kashruth. Kosher foods are those permitted under kashruth. Most foods are kosher. But certain animals, including pigs and all shellfish, are not.

Kashruth also describes how people must prepare and serve foods. For instance, it forbids eating meat and dairy together. So a hamburger can be kosher, while a cheeseburger cannot. Like Islamic law, kashruth requires Jews to kill livestock quickly and as painlessly as possible. Kashruth also requires Jews to drain, soak, or salt all the blood out of meat.

October 5, 2007

From the Pages of USA TODAY

Ind. farmer offers kill-it-yourself meat; International array of people come to buy, butcher goats

HAZELWOOD, Ind.—The morning sun is only beginning to peek over the horizon, but Tom Prince's farm 20 miles [32 km] west of Indianapolis is already abuzz.

Cars, pickups, minivans and taxicabs are parked next to a small metal-sided barn behind Prince's neatly kept farmhouse. Inside, the strains of a half-dozen languages echo in the background as a Muslim man kneels over a goat, says a brief prayer, then cuts the animal's throat. It's hard to imagine a greater cultural mishmash than the early morning gatherings that take place here every Friday and Saturday.

Since 1999, Prince has operated a self-service slaughterhouse that specializes in providing goat meat to the Indianapolis area's growing international community. His card reads "You Buy—You Kill—You Dress—You Take Home," and business is booming. Prince also sells lamb and sheep, but goats are the big seller.

Prince, 80, runs the facility from 7 a.m. to 1 p.m. every Friday and Saturday, selling an average of about 50 goats per weekend. In the weeks before Muslim and other religious holidays, he says, sales often double.

Prince's slow Southern drawl stands out from the languages spoken by customers who have found their way to Central Indiana from Morocco, Yemen, Nigeria, Kenya, Pakistan, Mexico and other places around the globe where goat is a dietary staple.

"When I moved out here in 1969, I bought four or five goats just for myself," says Prince, who developed his taste for goat as a child growing up in rural Tennessee during the Depression. "Then an African fellow came out and asked me if I'd sell him some. I sold him two, and he said he'd be back next week for two more, and that's what really got me started."

Prince says his business continues to grow—even though he doesn't advertise or have a website—thanks to word-of-mouth recommendations.

For some, butchering their own meat helps maintain a link to cultures they've left behind in Africa, Central America and the Middle East. Others,

Ahmed Awad *(left)*, a Muslim man who immigrated to the United States from Yemen, drags his newly killed goat to a table where he will clean it and prepare to take it home. This farm in Indiana caters to people who want to slaughter their own goat or sheep.

including the large number of Muslims who buy from Prince, prefer to kill and butcher the animals themselves to ensure that the food preparation standards of their faith are followed.

Prince said he doesn't know a lot about Islam, but he is savvy enough as a businessman to make sure the slaughterhouse meets their needs—including situating the killing table so it faces east toward Mecca.

Muslim customers such as Ahmed Awad, 37, of Indianapolis say they appreciate the nod to their faith. A native of Yemen, Awad has come to the slaughterhouse about once a month for the past year to get meat for his family.

—*Tim Evans*

These diners share a bowl of couscous and vegetables. Couscous is a popular wheat-based dish in parts of the Middle East. Eating out of the same large bowl or platter is a traditional Middle Eastern custom.

Many Middle Easterners and some Middle Eastern Americans, regardless of their religion, follow certain eating customs. They usually serve food from large platters in the middle of a table. Diners sit on the floor and eat with their right hands. Although everyone eats from the same platter, each diner eats only from the part of the platter directly in front of him or her. Diners also avoid pointing the soles of their feet directly at anyone. This act is considered bad luck as well as rude.

Barbecued Lamb

Barbecued lamb is popular in many Middle Eastern countries and in Middle Eastern families in the United States. Ask an adult to help with the grilling.

INGREDIENTS

½ cup olive oil
3 onions, grated
2 cloves garlic, crushed
½ teaspoon saffron (optional, may be expensive in U.S. grocery stores)
salt
black pepper
1 pound boneless lamb
6 medium tomatoes

PREPARATION

1. Make a marinade by mixing olive oil, onions, garlic, saffron, salt, and black pepper in a large bowl.
2. Cut the lamb into 1-inch cubes and mix it into the marinade. Cover the bowl, and refrigerate overnight.
3. The next day, thread the lamb pieces on long, thin metal skewers.
4. Thread whole tomatoes separately on another skewer. Brush with marinade.
5. Grill for 5 to 10 minutes on each side, turning often.
6. Serve hot with basmati rice, white rice, or on pita bread.

This recipe makes 6 servings.

FAMOUS MIDDLE EASTERN AMERICANS

Sama Alshaibi
(b. 1973) Artist Sama Alshaibi was born in Basra, Iraq, to an Iraqi father and Palestinian mother. When Alshaibi was twelve years old, her family emigrated from Iraq to the United States. She became a U.S. citizen and graduated from Columbia College in Chicago. She later received a master's degree in photography and media arts from the University of Colorado at Boulder. She has exhibited her photography and films around the world.

Catherine Bell
(b. 1968) Actress Catherine Bell was born in London, England, to an Iranian mother and Scottish father. After her parents divorced, Bell moved to California with her mother and became a U.S. citizen. She began acting in television commercials as a child. She later attended the University of California, Los Angeles, to study science. She left school so she could model and act full-time. From 1997 to 2005, she starred in the television show *JAG*. In 2006 she joined the cast of the television show *Army Wives*.

Michael DeBakey
(1908–2008) Michael DeBakey was one of the greatest heart surgeons in history. DeBakey was born in Lake Charles, Louisiana, to Lebanese immigrants. When he was still in medical school, he invented the roller pump. This device allows blood to continue flowing during heart operations. It made open-heart surgery possible. In 1939 DeBakey became one of the first scientists to link smoking and lung cancer. DeBakey continued practicing medicine until the day he died in 2008 at the age of ninety-nine.

Alber Elbaz
(b. 1961) Israeli-American fashion designer Alber Elbaz was born in Casablanca, Morocco, in northern Africa. His family moved to Israel when he was ten. He graduated from fashion design school in Israel and moved to the United States at the age of twenty-seven. Throughout the 1990s, he worked for top U.S. fashion houses, including Geoffrey Beene, Guy Laroche, and Yves Saint Laurent. In 2001 he became artistic director of Lanvin in Paris, one of the world's oldest fashion houses.

Chris Kattan

(b. 1970) Comedian Chris Kattan is Iraqi American. He was born in Sherman Oaks, California, and grew up on Bainbridge Island, Washington. Kattan and his father were both members of the Groundlings, a Los Angeles sketch comedy troupe. From 1995 to 2003, Kattan was a *Saturday Night Live* cast member. His recurring characters included Mr. Peepers, Mango, Azrael Abyss, and Doug Butabi of the Butabi Brothers. Kattan and Will Ferrell expanded their Butabi Brothers characters in the 1998 movie *A Night at the Roxbury*.

Ralph Nader

(b. 1934) Ralph Nader has been called the People's Crusader. He has spent his life fighting for consumer and civil rights in the United States. He was born to Lebanese immigrants in Connecticut. He became famous in 1965 when he published the book *Unsafe at Any Speed*. The book attacked the large U.S. auto companies and said they were knowingly building unsafe cars. His work led to many safety measures, such as the introduction of seat belts. Nader went on to wage similar crusades to reform other industries. He has also run for president four times.

Kathy Najimy

(b. 1957) Actress Kathy Najimy was born in San Diego, California, to Lebanese immigrants. Najimy has been successful onstage and in film and television. She played Sister Mary Patrick in the 1992 movie *Sister Act* and the 1993 sequel *Sister Act 2*. Najimy has also appeared on several television dramas, sitcoms, and game shows. She appeared on the show *Desperate Housewives* in 2009. She donates her game show winnings to causes such as ending domestic violence.

Donna Shalala

(b. 1941) Donna Shalala was born in Cleveland, Ohio, to Lebanese immigrants. She became the first Arab American presidential cabinet member when Bill Clinton appointed her secretary of health and human services in 1993. She served for eight years. Since 2001 she has been the president of the University of Miami in Coral Gables, Florida.

EXPLORE YOUR HERITAGE

Where did your family come from? Who are your relatives, and where do they live? Were they born in the United States? If not, when and why did they come here? Where did you get your family name? Is it German? Puerto Rican? Vietnamese? Something else? If you are adopted, what is your adoptive family's story?

By searching for the answers to these questions, you can begin to discover your family's history. And if your family history is hard to trace, team up with a friend to share ideas or to learn more about that person's family history.

Where to Start

Start with what you know. In a notebook or on your family's computer, write down the full names of the relatives you know about and anything you know about them—where they lived, what they liked to do as children, any awards or honors they earned, and so on.

Next, gather some primary sources. Primary sources are the records and observations of eyewitnesses to events. They include diaries; letters; autobiographies; speeches; newspapers; birth, marriage, and death records; photographs; and ship records. The best primary resources about your family may be in family scrapbooks or files in your home or in your relatives' homes. You may also find some interesting material in libraries, archives, historical societies, and museums. These organizations often have primary sources available online.

The Next Steps

After taking notes and gathering primary sources, think about what facts and details you are missing. You can then prepare to interview your relatives to see if they can fill in these gaps. First, write down any questions that you would like to ask them about their lives. Then ask your relatives if they would mind being interviewed. Don't be upset if they say no. Understand that some people do not like to talk about their pasts.

Also, consider interviewing family friends. They can often provide interesting stories and details about your relatives. They might have photographs too.

Family Interviews

When you are ready for an interview, gather your questions, a notepad, a tape recorder or camcorder, and any other materials you might need. Consider showing your interview subjects a photograph or a timetable of important events at the start of your interview. These items can help jog the memory of your subjects and get them talking. You might also bring U.S. and world maps to an interview. Ask your subjects to label the places they have lived.

Remember that people's memories aren't always accurate. Sometimes they forget information and confuse dates. You might want to take a trip to the library or look online to check dates and other facts.

Get Organized!

When you finish your interviews and research, you are ready to organize your information. There are many ways of doing this. You can write a history of your entire family or individual biographies of your relatives. You can create a timeline going back to your earliest known ancestors. You can make a family tree—a diagram or chart that shows how people in your family are related to one another.

If you have collected a lot of photographs, consider compiling a photo album or scrapbook that tells your family history. Or if you used a camcorder to record your interviews, you might even want to make a movie.

However you put together your family history, be sure to share it! Your relatives will want to see all the information you found. You might want to create a website or blog so that other people can learn about your family. Whatever you choose to do, you'll end up with something your family will appreciate for years to come.

MIDDLE EASTERN AMERICAN SNAPSHOT

This chart shows the five Middle Eastern countries from which the largest numbers of Middle Eastern Americans have come. It also shows the total number of people who have arrived in the United States from each country, the years they arrived in greatest numbers, and the top five states where they settled.

COUNTRY OF ORIGIN	TOTAL POPULATION U.S. CENSUS 2000	YEARS OF GREATEST IMMIGRATION	TOP FIVE STATES OF RESIDENCE (IN DESCENDING ORDER)
Lebanon	440,279	1900s–1920s	Michigan, California, Illinois, Ohio, Texas
Iran	338,266	1980s	California, Texas, Virginia, Illinois, Florida
Syria	142,897	1900s–1920s	Michigan, California, Illinois, Ohio, Texas
Egypt	142,832	1970s, 1990s	New Jersey, New York, California, Virginia, Texas
Israel	106,389	1980s	New York, New Jersey, Illinois, Florida, California

GLOSSARY

assimilate: to fit in with and adopt the ways of a new culture

choreographer: an artist who composes the steps to a dance

Christianity: a religion based on the life and teachings of Jesus. Christians believe that Jesus is the Son of God and that he suffered, died, and came back from the dead so that after death, their souls will go to heaven.

discrimination: unfair behavior toward others based on differences in age, race, gender, religion, and other differences

fast: to avoid eating or drinking for a period of time

generation: the average amount of time between the birth of parents and that of their children, or about twenty-five years. One generation is all the people born around the same time.

halal: a term often used in reference to food. Halal foods and preparation methods are those permitted by Islamic dietary law.

haram: a term often used in reference to food. Haram foods and preparation methods are those forbidden by Islamic dietary law.

immigrant: a person from one country who moves to live in another country

Islam: a religion based on the teachings of Muhammad, who was born in the A.D. 500s in Saudi Arabia. Muslims believe that Allah (God) is the only god and that Muhammad is God's prophet, or messenger. Islamic practice centers on faith, prayer, fasting, charity, and pilgrimage.

Judaism: the religion of the Jewish people, based on the belief in one God and the teachings of the Torah, the first five books of the Hebrew Bible. Among the Torah's central teachings are the Ten Commandments, which God gave to Moses.

kashruth: Jewish dietary law. Kosher foods, preparation, and serving methods are those permitted by kashruth.

Muslim: a follower of the religion of Islam

pilgrimage: a journey to worship at a holy place

persecution: inflicting suffering, harm, or death on someone, particularly a group of people based on their differences

prophet: a spiritual spokesperson who speaks or claims to speak for a divine being

Quran: the holy book of Islam, also sometimes spelled Koran

worship: to express devotion to a divine being, often during a formal service with other worshippers

SELECTED BIBLIOGRAPHY

Abinader, Elmaz. "Children of Al-Mahjar: Arab American Literature Spans a Century." *U.S. Society & Values*. February 2000. http://usinfo.org/zhtw/DOCS/ijse0200/abinader.htm (January 18, 2010).
This article traces the development of Arab American literature from the turn of the twentieth century to the present.

Arab American Institute. "Arab Americans." Arab American Institute. N.d. http://www.aaiusa.org/arab-americans (January 18, 2010).
This website includes demographic and census information about Arab Americans as well as research and updates on issues facing the Arab American community.

Benson, Kathleen, and Philip M. Kayal. *A Community of Many Worlds: Arab Americans in New York City*. Syracuse, NY: Syracuse University Press, 2002.
This book examines the unique experiences of Middle Eastern Americans living in New York City.

Brittingham, Angela, and G. Patricia de la Cruz. "We the People of Arab Ancestry in the United States: Census 2000 Special Reports." U.S. Census Bureau. March 2005. http://www.census.gov/prod/2005pubs/censr-21.pdf (December 14, 2009).
This special report provides a portrait of the Arab population in the United States.

Camarota, Steven A. "Immigrants from the Middle East: A Profile of the Foreign-Born Population from Pakistan to Morocco." Center for Immigration Studies. August 2002. http://www.cis.org/articles/2002/back902.html (January 18, 2010).
This article by the center's director of research discusses the history and demographics of Middle Eastern American immigrants as well as U.S. policy toward this group.

Marvasti, Amir B., and Karyn D. McKinney. *Middle Eastern Lives in America*. Lanham, MD: Rowman & Littlefield, 2004.
This book describes the experiences of Middle Eastern Americans and their many contributions to their new country.

Oweis, Fayeq. *Encyclopedia of Arab American Artists*. Westport, CT: Greenwood Publishing Group, 2008.
This book profiles more than fifty Arab American visual artists.

Reading Islam Project. "Ask about Islam." Reading Islam. 2010. http://www.islamonline.net/english/index.shtml (January 18, 2010).
This resource provides links to more than one thousand articles about Islam. It is part of a comprehensive website about the religion.

Shora, Nawar. *Arab-American Handbook: A Guide to the Arab, Arab-American and Muslim Worlds*. Seattle: Cune Press, 2008.
This reference book contains useful information about the cultures of Arab Americans and Muslims.

FURTHER READING AND WEBSITES

Arab American National Museum
http://www.arabamericanmuseum.org
Explore the world's largest museum devoted to Arab Americans with interactive features such as a virtual tour and an online catalog of available materials.

Easy Menu Ethnic Cookbooks series. Minneapolis: Lerner Publications Company, 2002–2005.
These easy-to-follow cookbooks weave together the history, culture, and cuisine of countries from around the world. To learn more about Middle Eastern cooking, readers can check out *Cooking the Israeli Way, Cooking the Lebanese Way, Cooking the Mediterranean Way, Cooking the Middle Eastern Way, Cooking the Turkish Way, Desserts around the World*, and *Holiday Cooking around the World*.

Holm, M. S. *How Mohammed Saved Miss Liberty*. New York: Sentry Books, 2007.
This novel tells the story of a family of Muslims in a small Ohio town dealing with the aftermath of the September 11, 2001, terrorist attacks.

Islam
http://www.kidspast.com/world-history/0171-islam.php
Explore the history of Islam in chapter eleven of an online world history textbook for kids.

January, Brendan. *The Iranian Revolution*. Minneapolis: Twenty-First Century Books, 2008.
Learn more about the 1979 revolution in Iran and how it led to a new wave of immigration to the United States. This book also explains how the revolution affected established Iranian Americans.

Kayyali, Randa A. *The Arab Americans*. Westport, CT: Greenwood Press, 2006.
Learn more about immigrants to the United States from the Arabian Peninsula. This book traces the history of Arab American immigration from the 1880s to the early 2000s.

Kort, Michael G. *The Handbook of the Middle East*. Minneapolis: Twenty-First Century Books, 2008.
To help young readers understand modern issues in the Middle East, this book explains the region's ancient civilizations, complex cultural makeup, and historical events that influence the current political climate.

Metcalf, Barbara Daly, ed. *Making Muslim Space in North America and Europe*. Berkeley: University of California Press, 1996.
This book contains many essays on Muslim life in the United States and other countries.

Nye, Naomi Shihab. *Habibi*. New York: Simon and Schuster, 1997.
This novel by an acclaimed Palestinian American author tells the story of a fourteen-year-old girl who moves with her family from Saint Louis, Missouri, to Jerusalem, Israel. The novel is set against the background of tension and violence between Israeli Jews and Palestinian Muslims.

Visual Geography Series. Minneapolis: Twenty-first Century Books, 2003–2011.
Each book in this series explains the land, history, government, people, culture, and economy of a different nation. The series includes titles on Egypt, Iran, Iraq, Israel, Jordan, Kuwait, Lebanon, Libya, Saudi Arabia, Syria, Turkey, Yemen, and more. Readers may also visit http://www.vgsbooks.com, the home page of the series, for late-breaking news and statistics.

Wormser, Richard. *American Islam: Growing Up Muslim in America*. New York: Walker and Company, 2002.
Learn more about Islam and the experiences of teenagers growing up Muslim in the United States. This book includes many quotes from young Muslim Americans describing their faith and their lives.

Yolen, Jane. *Milk and Honey: A Year of Jewish Holidays*. New York: Putnam Juvenile, 1996.
This beautifully illustrated book leads readers on a journey through the major Jewish holidays.

INDEX

Abdul, Paula, 20
Abinader, Elmaz, 13
actors, 21–23
Agassi, Andre, 30
Aggour, Yasser, 25
Al-Dhaher, Sabah, 25
Alshaibi, Sama, 70
Anka, Paul, 17
Arab-American Film Maker Award, 21
Arab-Israeli conflict, 40, 42–43
Arab-Israeli War, 5, 40
artists, 25, 70
arts and crafts, 24–25
assimilation into American culture, 35, 41, 44, 59
athletes. *See* sports

baseball, 31
basketball, 32
Bell, Catherine, 70
Blatty, William Peter, 12
butchers, 64–65, 66–67

camel racing, 27–28
carpets, Persian, 24–25
Chaldean Christians, 38
Christianity, 5, 36, 37–39; holidays of, 54–57; persecution and, 38, 39
Christmas, 54–56
clothing and modesty, 33, 34–35, 42
cooking. *See* food
Coptic Christians, 39

dance, 19–20
DeBakey, Michael, 70
Dhaher, Sabah Al-. *See* Al-Dhaher, Sabah
dietary restrictions, 64–65
discrimination: anti-Muslim, 22–23, 45; in Hollywood, 21–22, 23; for modest dress, 34–35

Easter, 56–57
Eastern Rite churches, 37–38, 54–57
Egypt, 5, 74
Eid al-Adha, 50–51
Eid al-Fitr, 49–50
Elbaz, Alber, 70

Fadhli, Hussam A., 25
falafel, 62; recipe, 63
falconry, 28–29
family history, researching, 72–73
Farr, Jamie, 21
FINCA (Foundation for International Community Assistance), 22–23
Flutie, Doug, 29
food, 59–69; common dishes, 60–61, 62; holiday meals, 47, 50, 51, 53, 57; restrictions, 64–65
football, 29, 31

genealogy, 72–73
George, Bill, 31
George, Jeff, 31
Gibran, Gibran Khalil, 10–11

Hanukkah, 52–53, 54–55
Hazo, Samuel, 12
holidays, 46–57; Christian, 54–57; Jewish, 52–53; meals for, 47, 50, 51, 53, 57; Muslim, 48–51; Nauruz, 46, 48
horse racing, 28

immigrants from the Middle East: common U.S. destinations of, 7, 38–39, 41, 44, 74; communities of, 47–48; U.S. population of, 5, 74
Iran, 5, 24–25, 74; food of, 61–63
Iranian Revolution, 5, 24–25, 61
Islam, 5, 36–37, 41–45; food restrictions, 64–65, 66–67; funerals, 51; holidays, 48–51
Israel, 5, 39–40, 74

Judaism, 5, 36, 39–41; holidays of, 52–53; persecution and, 17, 39, 40

Kattan, Chris, 71
Khaled, Khaled, 19
khaleegy, 20
Khalifa, Sam, 31
kosher foods, 65

Lahoud, Joe, 31
lamb recipe, 69
languages, 5, 6; learning English, 6–7; translators, 14–15
Lebanon, 5, 74; food of, 59–61
literature, 8–15

Maronite Church, 37–38
media, 8, 27
Middle Eastern countries, 5, 74
Mizrachi Jews, 40
Muhammad, 5, 37, 41
music, 16–19, 42–43
Muslims. *See* Islam

Nader, Ralph, 71
Najimy, Kathy, 71
Nauruz, 46, 48
Nazi Germany, 17, 39
Nye, Naomi Shihab, 11–12

Palestine, 14–15, 39–40, 42–43
Passover, 53
peace efforts, 42–43
Pen League, the, 9–11
poetry, 9–12
politicians, 71
Portman, Natalie, 22–23

Ramadan, 48–50
recipes: barbecued lamb, 69; falafel, 63
religion: charity in, 43, 49, 50, 54–55; Christianity, 5, 36, 37–39, 54–57; Islam, 5, 36–37, 41–45, 48–51; Judaism, 5, 36, 39–41, 52–55; persecution and, 17, 38, 39–40, 45; Sufism/mysticism, 19–20
Rihani, Ameen, 9
Rosh Hashanah, 52

Said, Edward, 14–15
Saint Barbara's Day, 57
Seikaly, Rony, 32
semazen, 19–20
September 11, 14, 15, 22–23, 45
Shalala, Donna, 71
Shalhoub, Tony, 21, 23
Simmons, Gene, 18
Simpson, Mona, 13
soccer, 27
sports, 27–35; women in, 33–35
Syria, 5, 74

tea, 61–62
television, 20–23, 70, 71
tennis, 30
terrorism, 23, 45

wars and conflicts: Arab-Israeli War, 5, 40; Iranian Revolution, 5, 24–25, 61
writers, 8–15

Yom Kippur, 52

Zappa, Frank, 17–18

PHOTO ACKNOWLEDGMENTS

The images in this book are used with the permission of: © Darren McCollester/Getty Images, pp. 3 (top), 4; © Jack Gruber/USA TODAY, pp. 3 (second from top), 8; © Darrell Gulin/Photographer's Choice/Getty Images, pp. 3 (third from top), 24; © World Sport Group/Getty Images, p. 3 (center); AP Photo/Rene Macura, pp. 3 (third from bottom), 49; © Bryan Smith/ZUMA Press, pp. 3 (second from bottom), 46; © iStockphoto.com/Juanmonino, pp. 3 (bottom), 60 (top); © James Marshall/The Image Works, p. 6; AP Photo/Paul Sancya, pp. 7, 65; © Art Directors & Trip/Alamy, p. 10; © Bob Daemmrich/The Image Works, p. 11; © Jeff Kravitz/FilmMagic/Getty Images, p. 12; Photo by Anthony Byers, Courtesy of Elmaz Abinader, p. 13; © iStockphoto.com/Atakan Sivgin, p. 16; © GAB Archive/Redferns/Getty Images, p. 17; © Dan MacMedan/USA TODAY, pp. 18, 20; © Owen Brewer/Sacramento Bee/ZUMA Press, p. 19; © Ann Clifford/DMI/Time & Life Pictures/Getty Images, p. 21; © Dimitrios Kambouris/WireImage/Getty Images, p. 23; Courtesy of Hussam A. Fadhli, MD, p. 25; © Lifestock/Taxi/Getty Images, p. 26; © Chris Jackson/Getty Images, p. 28; © Robert Hanashiro/USA TODAY, p. 29; © Robert Deutsch/USA TODAY, pp. 30, 55; AP Photo, p. 31; © Porter Binks/USA TODAY, p. 32; © Blend Images/SuperStock, p. 33; © Sandy Huffaker/Getty Images, p. 36; © Mark Richards/ZUMA Press, p. 40; © Melanie Stetson Freeman/The Christian Science Monitor/Getty Images, p. 44; AP Photo/Emile Wamsteker, p. 56; © iStockphoto.com/John Peacock, p. 58; © Food and Drink/SuperStock, p. 60 (bottom); © Bon Appetit/Alamy, p. 61; © Dave Bartruff/CORBIS, p. 62; © Sam Riche, The Indianapolis Star/USA TODAY, p. 67; © Floris Leeuwenberg/The Cover Story/CORBIS, p. 68; Photo by Marvin Gladney, Courtesy of Sama Alshaibi, p. 70 (top); AP Photo/Jeff Christensen, p. 70 (second from top); AP Photo/David J. Phillip, p. 70 (second from bottom); © Andrew H. Walker/Getty Images, p. 70 (bottom); © Jordan Strauss/WireImage/Getty Images, p. 71 (top); © Tali Greener, Norwich Bulletin/USA TODAY, p. 71 (second from top); © Kevin Winter/Getty Images, p. 71 (second from bottom); © H. Darr Beiser/USA TODAY, p. 71 (bottom); © Todd Strand/Independent Picture Service, pp. 72–73.

Front Cover: © Randy Duchaine/Alamy (top); © Terry Vine/Blend Images/Getty Images (bottom left); AP Photo/Amr Nabil (bottom right).

ABOUT THE AUTHOR

Children's and YA author Sandy Donovan has written numerous titles, including *Running for Office: A Look at Political Campaigns*, *Iranians in America*, and three titles in the USA TODAY Cultural Mosaic series. Donovan is a graduate of the Humphrey Institute of Public Policy at the University of Minnesota and lives in Minneapolis, Minnesota.